Falling for Dez

Chrissie Clay

Chrissie Clay

Also by Chrissie Clay

Brooklyn Bridge Bae

The Truth about Marriage: 8 Principles for Sustaining
a Christian Marriage

Virginia is for Lovers: Book 1

Virginia is for Lovers: Book 2 (Fall 2025)

Contents

Playlist

Apple Music

Spotify

Before You Read

Hey!

I hope you're ready to dive into the world of Justin and Dezzy! Before you read though, please know that **this is a spin-off of my first novel, *Brooklyn Bridge Bae*.** While you don't need to read *Brooklyn Bridge Bae* before reading *Falling for Dez,* know that references to and spoilers for that novel exist in this one.

On that note, thanks for picking up this sweet and short love story. I hope you enjoy the unexpected budding love between Justin and Dezzy. Don't forget to enjoy accompanying playlist. Whether it be questions, comments, or anything else, I'd enjoy hearing from you. ☺

Chapter 1: Justin

February 14, 2015

"You doin' what now?" I ask my best friend, Romeo Raymond.

He chuckles loudly, causing me to turn down the volume in my BMW X6. Romeo and I have been best friends since freshman year at Georgia State in 2003. I'm originally from Kansas, and when his mom found out my parents were having trouble picking me up for Christmas break, she invited me to spend the holidays with them. Since then, Romeo's family has been my second family, down to even giving me my own house key.

"I'm making dinner for Jane. It's Valentine's, so I thought a candle-lit home-cooked meal would be romantic," Romeo explains as I circle the block, hoping for an off-the-street parking spot.

"That woman has you whipped. You won't catch me making dinner for some broad."

"That's why you're going to end up alone. Women are just toys to you. As soon as you get bored, you block her and go shopping for someone else."

I chuckle, unable to deny the truth. A car pulls out of a spot then, and I quickly swoop into the space. "Man, falling in love is not in my plans. I'm too busy trying to make a career change."

"Then why are you going on a date tonight?"

"Because changing careers is stressful. I need a muscle relaxer."

"Relaxing your muscle isn't what you have planned for tonight," Rome says before the two of us bust out laughing.

"Whatever, bro. I'm at my destination. I'll holla at you tomorrow."

Rome hangs up, and I reach into the backseat to grab the bouquet of flowers that has me late in the first place. If I didn't care so much about being suave, then I would've skipped the flowers, but it is Valentine's Day.

Resting the bouquet in my lap, I pull down the visor and look myself over. My face is clean, and my teeth are white. After putting ChapStick on, I grab my car brush and brush my waves before combing my facial hair. I usually keep a clean face for work, but I've been flirting with the idea of growing it out. People call me a pretty boy, but I don't care. There's nothing wrong with self-grooming. In my opinion, more men should take it up.

Satisfied with my appearance, I grab my leather jacket and get out of the SUV. Catching a glimpse of my reflection while walking to the restaurant, I stop and fix my collar that's half up and half down. I also adjust my black turtleneck and silver chains to my liking. I touch my ear, ensuring my earring is still there, and then resume walking to Groove's.

"Welcome to Groove's Restaurant and Bar. How may I help you?" the host asks when I step in. He's wearing a black button-up shirt with black slacks.

Located in Midtown Atlanta, Groove's has been around for about three years. The walls are white, but all the décor is black. Black glossy tiles on the floor and black tables and chairs. There isn't much to catch the eye, but customers come here because the food and drinks are good.

The restaurant is dimly lit with multicolored lights throughout, and music plays loudly as if we're in a club. Personally, I avoid this place because I can't stand the stifling, rosy, perfume aroma. When I go to a restaurant, I like to smell food—not the woman's section in a department store.

"I have a reservation for two under the name Campbell."

The host searches through a black book before looking at me and smiling. "Your table is ready. Is your guest here?"

"She isn't here yet?" I ask, surprised. "Can you give me a minute to call her?"

The host nods, and I step to the side to call Lisa. Her phone rings a few times before going to voicemail. I call back again, but this time her phone goes straight to voicemail. She texts me then.

> Lisa: *Sorry. Can't make it tonight. I'll make it up to you soon. XOXO*

Sucking my teeth, I block her and return to the host.

"Scratch the reservation. I'll just sit at the bar," I say, walking away before he can tell me anything else.

I've never been stood up before, and despite being a womanizer, as some label me, I've never stood anyone up. If I have to cancel a date, I let the woman know in advance. The bar is pretty empty, unsurprisingly. Everyone is seated with a date. Tossing the bouquet on the counter, I pull a stool out and sit. The bartender finishes taking a customer's order on the other side of the counter before approaching me.

"What can I get for you?"

"I need two shots. One rum, and the other tequila."

The bartender looks at me, suspiciously. "You sure you want to mix those two?"

"Yes," I say, pulling out my phone and checking my email.

"Coming up," he says, walking away.

I usually don't work outside of the office or court, but I'm desperate to forget about my current dilemma. There aren't any new emails, so I scroll through Twitter to see what's been going on in the world.

"Justin?" someone calls.

Looking up, I see Dez, Romeo's little sister. Everyone calls her Dezzy, but much like her actual name, Desdemona, there are too many syllables, so I call her Dez. She's wearing a smile, but it's obvious she's stunned to see me here.

"Hey. What are you doing here?" I ask as she approaches.

"I work here," she says, matter-of-factly.

I then notice her attire. She's wearing a black button-up shirt, just like the host, but with a knee-length skirt instead of slacks. On her feet are high-top black and white Nike Dunks.

"Since when?" I ask in disbelief.

She rolls her eyes. "Bruh, I've been working here since they opened up my sophomore year of college." Despite being from New York, Dez has a Southern accent and uses all of Atlanta's colloquialisms.

"I thought you worked at a chicken place."

"Shows how much you pay attention to me," she says before sticking her tongue out.

"At least I know you work at a restaurant."

"What are you doing here?" she asks, sitting beside me. "That's right, it's Valentine's Day. What unlucky woman have you seduced into hanging with you tonight?"

"I'm the unlucky one. I got stood up," I admit as the bartender returns with my two shots.

"You plan on sitting here and getting drunk for the rest of the night?" Dez asks, giving me a disappointed look.

I shrug. "I can walk home from here if I'm unfit to drive."

"What did you order?"

"Rum," I say, pointing to it, "and tequila."

Nodding, she picks up the glass with tequila.

"What are you doing? You can't drink," I say, alarmed.

She scoffs before glancing at the bartender. "How old do you think I am, Jus? I been old enough to drink. Rob and I take shots quite often."

"Just don't tell our manager," The bartender, Rob, says before walking away.

"I'm about to graduate, but you don't think I'm old enough to drink?" Dez asks.

A lightbulb goes off then. She'll be turning 24 in August.

"That's right. I got you that great early graduation gift for Christmas, and you got me a shotty Bluetooth speaker."

"It was thirty dollars," she defends.

The camera I bought for Dez was on sale for a little over $800. Dez's mom and I were doing last-minute Christmas shopping when she spotted the camera. She told me Dez had been asking for it since her birthday, but because they are saving up to surprise her with a car for graduation, they couldn't afford to get her the camera. I knew her mom wasn't subconsciously trying to ask me to purchase it.

I bought the camera because Dez deserved it after her hard work. During her third year of college, she switched majors from business accounting to journalism and digital media. It shocked everyone, including her academic advisor who told her she'd have to remain in school longer. Dez didn't care, and now she's on track to graduate Magna Cum Laude in May from Georgia State.

"Let's just drink," I say, raising my glass to hers.

We toast, and she takes the shot straight. Guess she isn't a little girl anymore. I take mine back too, and we both slam our glasses on the curved, space-colored counter before looking at each other and chuckling.

"I need five more of these," I tell Rob when he returns.

"Justin!" Dez objects.

"What? You took my tequila, so I need five more of these to compensate."

"My shift is over, and I'm hungry. Let's go get something to eat," Dez demands.

Sighing, I pull out my wallet. "Fine," I agree, leaving a twenty on the counter and standing up.

Dez throws a small, lime green bookbag on and walks to the exit. Grabbing the bouquet, I follow her.

"Where do you wanna eat?" I ask as we stand outside of Groove's.

"Tropical Breeze. It's a lounge not too far from here."

"I know where it is. You okay with walking?" I ask as a couple tries to maneuver around us to get inside Groove's. Placing my hand on Dez's back, I pull her toward me and away from the entrance. She stiffens.

"Sure, but can I ask you something first?"

"Don't worry, I'll pay. I know what it's like to be a struggling college student."

She hits my chest. It hurts more than anticipated, causing me to remember that I've been slacking on working out since Rome moved to New York.

"I'm not talking about money, but you were going to pay anyway because I'm a lady."

"Then what's up?" I ask, looking at her.

Standing beside me, she hangs her head. I turn to face her fully. I've known her for twelve years and have never seen her scared to say or ask anything. "Since it's Valentine's Day, I wanna go to Tropical Breeze with you as your date."

"What?" I ask, confident I didn't hear her correctly.

Dez glances at the flowers in my hand before looking straight ahead.

"To be honest with you, Justin, I've had a crush on you since tenth grade."

"On *me*? Dez, you picked arguments with me for no reason. You always targeted me in Smash Bros. and *Mario Party*. Whenever I came over during college, you would hug Rome and then ask why he brought me along. You've never shown any interest in me."

"It was a small crush," she says, raising her voice. "You're my brother's best friend, so you were like a brother to me by extension. So, I suffocated those thoughts about you whenever they surfaced. But then you started coming over more, especially after Romeo got married and moved out. We spent more time together, and I got to know you outside of Romeo. Then I realized I don't like you as a brother; I just like you."

I stare at her, flummoxed. There's no way I'm hearing her correctly. I've only ever seen Dez as Rome's sister. I've never flirted with or done anything inappropriate to her.

"Getting that camera for Christmas sent me over the moon," Dez continues. "Then when I found out it was from you, I was simultaneously overjoyed and sadden. I felt like crap for just getting you a speaker."

"You should've felt like crap for getting it anyway," I manage to say. "But the speaker's not that bad. I've used it a few times."

She chuckles softly before saying, "I really appreciate the camera, Justin." She glances at me. "Tonight, I want to be your Valentine, and I want this to be a date." She takes a deep breath before looking into my eyes. "I don't want you to see me as your best friend's little sister. I want you to see me for the beautiful woman that I am." Then she flashes a smile. "Unless you don't think I'm beautiful."

Silently staring at her, I reflect on what she's told me. Dez is six years younger than Rome and me, so I've never looked at her romantically. Forcing my brain to separate her from Rome, however, I do see her as a beautiful woman. Light-skinned and five-eight, her hair stops just below her ears. It's loosely curled with a middle-part tonight. She has brown eyes and high cheekbones. She's tall and slender—not the type of chick I usually go for, but beautiful, nonetheless. Breaking eye contact, I look at the cars driving by in the street. I am dressed up, and she is hungry, so why not?

"Will you be my Valentine, Dez?" I ask, offering her the bouquet of flowers.

Her face instantly lights up.

"Yes!" she says, taking the flowers. "Let's go eat. I'm starved."

Taking her by the hand, we begin walking. Tropical Breeze is a Guyanese lounge that serves Guyanese and other Caribbean dishes. Soca music escapes to the streets when I open the door for us to enter. Stepping inside, I feel like we've been transported to an island in the Caribbean. Every Caribbean flag hang in the restaurant, going along the top of the walls. On the walls themselves are paintings of people lounging on the beach, dancing in a club, and eating at a restaurant.

We're seated immediately. Dez orders chicken curry with roti and a mango margarita, while I order jerk chicken with plantain and rice and peas.

"If you like rum, then this is the place to get some. Start off with a rum and Coke," she suggests.

I give the waitress my order, specifying that I'd like to try the Guyanese El Dorado rum. While waiting on our food, Dez and I make small talk about our day. She hung out with some friends before coming into work. I got a haircut and carwash before stopping by the cleaners. Then I played video games until it was time to get ready for my date that stood me up.

"Serves you right, for all the hearts you've broken in the past," Dez teases, sipping her margarita.

"And you haven't broken any hearts?"

She smiles deviously. "Nope," she answers, looking off into the distance.

Of course she has. She was mean to me despite finding me attractive. I can only imagine what she did to men she didn't even remotely like. Our food arrives just as she finishes telling me about her classes. It's her last semester, so she only has two. A relatively light load compared to the semesters she had to take five.

"A toast to you almost being finished with school. Finally," I tease, raising my glass.

"If we're toasting, let's get some real drinks," Dez says before waving at our waitress.

She orders a round of tequila, and we toast as soon as they arrive. She asks the waitress to bring two more rounds before diving into her food.

"Have you used the camera yet?" I ask, eating some chicken.

Dez sighs. "No. I've bought a tripod and protective case for it. I've taken it with me on several outings, but nothing has been spectacular enough to capture yet. I've been using my old camera–you know, the one I saved up for and bought my sophomore year of college."

"Which sophomore year... the real one or the one when you still wanted to be an accountant?"

Laughing, she playfully hits my hand. "Anyway, maybe I'll wait until graduation to use it. That moment should be special enough."

We don't say much else as we eat. We make occasional eye contact, and our hands brush past each other a few times, but that's it.

"I'm not going to be able to finish this," Dez says, sitting up and rubbing her stomach. A tiny bulge appears, showing she's bloated.

Chuckling, I sit up too. "They do give you your money's worth of food here. Let's get to-go boxes," I suggest.

"Sure," she says, reaching for the shots we haven't taken yet. She slides two glasses to me before sliding two toward herself.

"Can't leave without finishing these."

I give her a suspicious look. "Are you trying to get drunk?" I refrain from saying I'm not on babysitter duty tonight. "Do you know your limit?"

She laughs. "If you cared about my drinking habits so much, you should've been lecturing me my freshman year. Since then, I've thrown up enough times to know my limit, and I'm now smart enough to not go past it. I'm not even tipsy."

"Fine," I say, giving in. "But the moment you start staggering, I'm finna—"

"Finna what? Drag me to my parents' house and tell them I've been a bad girl?" She laughs.

We both know I wouldn't do that. There's been times Dez has been in the city with her friends, called me for a ride, and I've taken them to wherever they were going. She never seemed drunk, and I figured she called because it was late, and they didn't feel safe riding with anyone else. She knows I'll take care of her.

"Let's go," I say, raising my glass.

We finish both shots, pack up our food, and leave. I keep a close eye on Dez as we head to my SUV. She's walking straight and isn't slurring—which is good. I guess she does know her limit.

"You want me to drop you off at your dorm, or are you going to a friend's house?" I ask, tugging on her lime green bookbag.

She stops walking, faces me, and wraps her arms around me.

"Can I come back to your place tonight?" Dez asks, gazing into my eyes.

My body stiffens, despite my heart racing. Removing one arm from around me, Dez tucks some hair behind her right ear, revealing four piercings, stands on her tippy toes, and kisses me. It's a light peck, but it's enough to make me wrap my arms around her waist and pull her closer. Kissing her back, I taste the strawberry of whatever lip gloss she's wearing before gently parting her lips and taking her bottom lip in mine. I stop then. She looks at me, confused.

"I guess you can come over," I whisper.

She smiles and lets me go. I open the passenger door for her, and after she's inside and buckled up, I walk to my side and get in. Dez turns on the radio and starts singing along to the R&B playing. I join in, trying to forget about the kiss we shared. Trying to forget about how soft her lips are. Trying to forget that we're currently headed to my condo... trying to forget that she's Romeo's sister.

Within twelve minutes, we're in the parking deck getting out of the car. I lead her to the deck's elevator and hit sixteen on the panel.

"Penthouse? I didn't know you got it like that," she says, impressed.

I chuckle. "You don't believe I'm a successful divorce lawyer?"

"I do now. I guess Rome wasn't just bragging on you because you're his friend."

I stare at the door, wondering what exactly Romeo would think about Dez coming to my condo. I only have one bed. There's a couch, but I have no idea how comfortable it is to sleep on. The elevator finally opens, and we step off. I lead Dez to my door, and she enters as soon as I unlock it. I hear the flicker of her turning on all the lights as she runs down the hallway. I follow her trail, turning off unnecessary lights, like the hallway one. Just because I'm well-off doesn't mean I like wasting money.

My condo has a very open concept, so I see Dez going from room to room even though I'm walking into the kitchen. She opens the bathroom door and praises me for having a rain showerhead and glass shower doors. Zipping out of the bathroom, she opens a hall closet, revealing my smart washer and dryer set. She complains about me giving into consumerism because I have such sophisticated tech before going into the living room and opening the floor-length blinds.

"Wow," she gasps. "You have such a beautiful view of Midtown. Why do you ever leave?"

"Because it's loud," I say, chuckling and turning toward the fridge.

Taking our leftovers out of the Tropical Breeze to-go bag, I place Dez's own on the left and mine on the right of the middle shelf. The condo's suspiciously quiet. Closing the fridge, I see Dez in the kitchen, staring at me.

"What's up?" I ask, walking to the kitchen sink to wash my hands.

"Thanks for letting me spend the night."

"No problem," I say, drying my hand on a dishtowel. *This is definitely going to be a problem.*

My phone starts vibrating in my pants pocket. Tossing the towel on the counter, I reach into my pocket and pull the phone out. Before I can see who's calling, however, Dez takes the phone from me and puts it back in my pocket. Puzzled, I look at her, ready to ask why she did that. Rather than opening my mouth, I watch as Dez hops up and sits on the counter. She pulls my turtleneck, causing me to walk to her so she won't stretch my shirt. When I'm close enough, she wraps her legs around me and starts kissing me.

My phone starts vibrating again, but I'm too caught up in Dez now. My arms are around her waist, and her hands are under my shirt, wrapped around my torso. I no longer taste her strawberry lip gloss, but rather the mango margarita she had, the curry and roti she declared was off the chain, and the shots of tequila we had before leaving.

Damn.

Chapter 2: Dezzy

Justin's kisses are like a remedy I never knew I needed. His lips are soft, and he holds me like I'm the most fragile jewel in the world. Hoisting me from the counter, he takes me down the hallway leading to his room. He uses one hand to draw the blinds back while holding me with the other. I'm surprised by his strength, but I shouldn't be since he was once a gym head.

His lips move from my mouth to my neck as he walks across the room. He gently rests me on the bed and stares at me. I'm about to ask what's wrong when I realize his look is one of awe; I must look devastatingly beautiful by moonlight. Smiling, I tug at his belt. He bites his bottom lip before opening his top drawer and taking out a condom.

Of course he has condoms; he is known for being a playboy after all. But I cast all of that out.

Tonight is about me and him. He takes his turtleneck off, and my body produces an involuntary "Mmm." I've seen him without a shirt plenty of times, as he's travelled with us on many family vacations, and seeing it now elicits the same feelings I was never permitted to act on.

Justin smirks and drops his pants. My eyes widen and my heart rate increases, but I'm no punk. I unbutton my shirt, and his awe returns as he takes in my powder blue bra. I stand up to untuck the shirt from my skirt, but he wraps an arm around my waist.

"I'll take care of that," he whispers before kissing just below my ear.
A chill runs down my spine. "Hold this for me." He slips the condom
between my fingers before using one hand to unzip my skirt, and the other
to take off my shirt.

His movements are so calculated, as if he's done this a plethora of times.
This will be my first, so I hope he's gentle. While picking me up, he
unhooks my bra and lays me on the bed. He kisses me from my lips to my
breasts, and down my torso. He stops just above my navel.

"When did you get this?" he asks, kissing around my navel butterfly ring.

I chuckle. "Freshman year."

He puts his hands under me and pushes my waist toward his face.

"Drinking." He kisses my left thigh. "Piercings." He kisses the right. "You
just misbehaved your entire freshman year, didn't you?"

"Wait until you see my tattoo," I tease.

He raises an eyebrow and looks at me. "What tattoo?"

Smirking, I open the condom and hand it to him. "You'll have to spot it
for yourself."

***

The sun wakes me the following day. I'm lying on his chest, and his arms
are wrapped around me. I don't move, wanting to enjoy this feeling for as
long as I can. Last night was magical, almost as if I were a princess in a fairy
tale. Justin was the perfect prince, ever so gentle and rewarding.

He kisses me on the forehead before caressing my back. I smile; glad he
has no remorse about last night. He reaches to the side of the bed, and
when I hear his belt buckle jingle, I figure he is looking for his phone. He
checks it, and then sits up, causing me to sit up as well. I'm stunned that he's
calling someone now, so I sit beside him, waiting to see who is important

enough for a call as soon as he wakes up.

"You there, bro?" Justin asks. I freeze: why is he talking to Romeo? Justin is an only child, and Romeo is the only person he considers a brother. I can't hear anything my brother is saying, so I can only rely on Justin's replies.

"I ran into—"

I hit him, and he looks at me. I have no regrets about last night, but I surely don't want my big brother to know I had sex. Justin gives me an apologetic look before resting his hand on my thigh. I can't make out much from Justin's responses, so I stretch, preparing to get out of bed. I groan as I run my hands through my hair; I already know it's a mess because I didn't tie it down last night.

Romeo's request must have something to do with a divorce decree because Justin vows to go into work. He gets off the phone and places it on the nightstand.

"Good morning," I greet, smiling at him.

He gives me a dismal look, and my heart stops. Is he having regrets?

"Good morning, Dez," he replies, forcing himself to smile. "I apologize. I don't usually make calls first thing in the morning, but I had to after seeing how many times Rome called."

Exhaling in relief, I feel my heart pumping again. "What's going on with him? I only heard bits and pieces," I say.

"He said he texted you. Donna is claiming—" Just stops abruptly.

"She's claiming what?"

"Client confidentiality."

"You can't tell me even though Romeo's my brother?"

"Especially because he's your brother," Justin says, taking his hand off me. "But I can't stop you from checking your phone and drawing your own conclusions."

Nodding, I get out of bed, naked.

"You uhh…" He trails off. He's blushing when I face him, causing me to smirk.

"I what?"

His eyes fight to stay on my face, but it's a losing battle. "You can wear my robe," he offers.

I chuckle. "No need. I'm perfectly comfortable. Besides," I say, glancing at the open window shades, "no one can see us way up here."

I turn to walk to the living room, but I catch him licking his lips before I leave. My phone is on the kitchen counter where I left it. I see messages from my girls, notifications from social media, and finally, a message from Romeo. I click on it.

> **Big Bro: Hey. Do I have any mail at the house? Specifically, from the magistrate court.**

> **Me: Not home but will be in a little while. I'll let you know.**

"What shenanigans is Donna up to now?" I ask, crossing the threshold of the bedroom. "She must not believe the divorce is final," I say, glancing at Justin.

He's now in basketball shorts and slides, standing in front of a chest of drawers. He looks at me and starts blushing again.

"Dez, please put something on," he urges. His tone is gentle.

Chuckling, I stand beside him. He takes my body in, captivated just like he was last night.

"I'm going to shower and head to Decatur. Romeo sent me on a mission of my own."

"Let me know if you need anything," he says, gazing into my eyes.

Is he talking about my shower needs or life ones? Ensnared in the trap set by his hazel eyes, it's difficult to discern his intended meaning.

"I will," I say, walking away.

I retrieve my lime green bag from the living room before heading to the bathroom. Large, white tiles line the floor. There's an illuminated mirror hanging above the white floating bathroom vanity. I grab a towel and washcloth from the linen closet, hang them in their appropriate locations, and then adjust the water to the temperature of my liking.

Once in, the wall panel sprays water on my back and torso, hitting all my pressure points. The rain showerhead drenches me from head to toe, causing my once flat-ironed hair to revert to the natural s-curl pattern I've had all my life.

Pumping some of his suspicious-looking body wash onto my washcloth, I replay his last words. Whether it was late-night-car rides, "please send me some money" texts, or pointless phone calls, Justin has always been there for me. Especially after Romeo married Donna and moved to Gwinnett; even more when Rome got divorced and moved back to Brooklyn.

Since high school I've fantasized about Justin being my dream guy–my prince charming. But I know his perspective on women, so as I lather with the washcloth, I replay our remarkable night once more, and as the water rinses the soap off my body and flushes it down the drain, I release every possibility of Justin and I being anything more than friends who had a one-night stand.

Chapter 3: Justin

February 16, 2015

S tanding, I loosen and pull off my tie. It's fifteen minutes to closing, but since there aren't any more appointments, I plan on closing early. I glance at my desk calendar to see what's scheduled for tomorrow before walking out of my office. My office is in a one-story suite I'm renting in Downtown Atlanta. It has a reception area—Cordelia's office—my office, a conference room, and two bathrooms. Cordelia is my secretary, assistant, notary, and any other business personnel I need her to be. She graduated with a B.A. in Paralegal Studies the same time I graduated from law school.

She took it upon herself to apply for a job, though I wasn't even hiring. It had only been two weeks since I signed the lease, and there she was beckoning for an interview. It's been three years since then, and we've been the best two-person crew since. Much like the initiative she took in applying for a nonexistent job, she decorated the suite without asking my input. I appreciated the gesture and reimbursed her with interest after we got our first client.

"We're closed," I tell Cordelia, stopping at her desk.

"I just need to email these documents to a client, and then I'll shut everything down. How did it go with Romeo's case?"

Cordelia knows Romeo from when he used to drop by when he lived in

Georgia.

"I called Donna's lawyer out on his BS. He purposely didn't send me the paperwork about the child, but I filed a report against him. Aside from that, Romeo's going to have to come next month for a court appearance where this will all come to an end."

"I should have followed up. My bad, Mr. Campbell."

"Don't beat yourself up about it. I should've been looking out for it too," I say before heading down the hall to the restroom. And I would have been following up with the judge every day if I thought more than just a signature was needed. Donna planting a baby on Romeo right before the divorce is finalized is toxic, but she's always been conniving and malicious.

While washing my hands, I hear the suite door open and close. Assuming Cordelia left for the day, I dry my hands on a paper towel before exiting.

"Mr. Campbell isn't seeing any more clients today. I can take your information down and have him reach out to you tomorrow," Cordelia says.

I check the time on my watch. There's less than ten minutes left before we officially close, but she's right; I'm not seeing any more clients today.

"Mr. Campbell may not, but Justin is. He's expecting me."

Is that Dez? What is she doing here?

"*Justin* has already fulfilled his appointments for the day, so you better leave before I have you escorted out," Cordelia rebuts.

"I can talk to him with or without an appointment. I don't need your permission to see him."

"I will call the cops on you if you walk past this desk," Cordelia warns.

"And I guarantee that if you call the cops, you'll be the one looking foolish, not me."

I walk into the reception area then.

"What is going on here?" I ask, looking at both women in their faces.

Cordelia's face is hard, and her lips are pursed. "I'm about to throw this little girl out, but—"

"First off, I'm a grown woman. Just because I'm younger than *you* doesn't mean I'm a little girl," Dez says, stepping to Cordelia.

Cordelia drops her purse, and I pull Dez behind me.

"Y'all need to settle down," I say, my tone as serious as the ass whuppin' one of them was going to receive.

They both exhale, and I let Dez go.

"Dez, this is Cordelia, my right hand at work, and on some days my left too." I move to the side so the women can make eye contact, but they're both too captivated by the fluorescent lights to look at each other. "Cordelia, this is Desdemona, my..." I look at Dez. What am I supposed to call her? My lover from a one-night stand? "Cordelia, Dez is allowed to see me as long as I'm not in a meeting or on a conference call."

"I told you," Dez spouts out.

"Hold up," I say, looking at her. "If you're going to be visiting my place of work, then you're going to have to respect Cordelia. She is vital in operating my practice, and I need her here. She means a lot to me, and I can't have her quitting just because you have an attitude."

"Fine, why don't you just go be with her?" Dez suggests, walking toward the exit.

I grab Dez's hand as Cordelia lets out a hearty laugh. I glance at Cordelia, and her laughter ends.

"If Dez comes, regardless of the time, please let me know," I tell her.

"Fine," Cordelia says before picking up her purse and heading to the restroom.

I lead a pouting Dez to my office, where I begin straightening up my desk.

"I'm sorry for causing a ruckus out there."

"I'm not the one you should be apologizing to," I say, putting my computer to sleep.

"I'm not apologizing to whatever her name is."

"Cordelia," I remind.

"You don't have a cute nickname for her?"

"I take my job seriously, Dez. I'm very professional at work."

She rolls her eyes.

"What are you doing here, anyway?" I ask. "You've never visited me at work before... and you haven't hit my line."

I was originally worried about protecting her feelings, but not hearing from her in over 24 hours had me feeling like the dates I blocked after dropping them home. Dez locks eyes with me and smirks.

"I didn't realize that was an issue for you. You love 'em once and move on, right? I know better than to get attached to you," she explains, sitting on my desk.

"That's not what I would've done to you," I admit as we maintain eye contact.

"Why not?" she asks, surprised.

I shrug. Was I to tell her that she's been on my mind all day and all day yesterday too?

"You're different. I wasn't looking for a relationship with those other girls."

"Are you looking for one now?" she asks, her voice barely a whisper. "Because I am."

After gathering my keys and briefcase, I stand in front of her. "You want to be in a relationship with me?"

She uses my shirt to pull me between her legs. *Must be a kink of hers.*

"How many times do I have to repeat this? Yes, I want to be in a relationship with you. I want us to date exclusively."

My phone vibrates then. Taking it out of my pocket, I see a Twitter message from Lisa.

> *Lisa: Can I see you tonight? Forgive me, and I'll make it worth your while.*

I block Lisa's account and drop the phone in my pocket. She and I have only hooked up twice, but she isn't anything to write home about.

"Don't block her just because I'm here, especially if you plan on taking her up on the offer."

I suck my teeth. "Lisa knew all day that she was not going to make it to dinner last night, but she allowed me to show up to the restaurant and look like a clown. I'm never speaking to her again."

"That's cold," Dez comments.

"Dating me wouldn't feel weird to you?"

"Why should it?"

"Because I'm six years older than you."

"Five years and eight months."

"You're about to graduate college and get your footing in life. There's a lot for you to experience and do."

"Based on how shocked you were about my piercing and tattoo, there's a lot I've experienced that you know nothing about."

She's right. Just because I stayed within my comfort zone until I got my bachelor's doesn't mean she has to also.

"I've never dated someone as young as you, so I can't even compute how compatible we'll be."

"I've never dated someone as old as you, so I can't imagine how many throwbacks you'll play for me as you talk about how great music used to be in the olden days."

I frown at her, and she chuckles.

"Wouldn't dating resolve that issue?" she asks. "I know my feelings for you. The only thing that could destroy them is if you say you want nothing to do with me romantically, or if we date and realize that we're not a good fit."

"I'm your brother's best friend."

"That's your fault. You had four years in college to drop him but didn't."

I chuckle. "You've had a lot of time to think about this."

She flashes a smile, the same one from Saturday night when she confessed her feelings. Her eyes are closed, and her smile is malleable, showing that depending on my response, her mouth can easily evolve into a real smile or devolve into a disappointed frown. I do have mixed feelings about dating Dez.

I usually only date older women, I've never dated a friend, and I can't fathom what Romeo, or his family will think about our relationship. But I had a great date with her on Saturday. Bringing her home was unexpected but very enjoyable. Though it's small, a part of me wants to see where a relationship would lead.

I move closer, and her smile brightens. Caressing her face, and looking into her eyes, I say, "I'm not trying to fall in love, Dez."

She pulls my face to hers. "I'm not asking you to fall in love; just fall for me." She kisses me, and I miss her lips more than I realize.

"Have a good evening... Mr. Campbell," Cordelia says, walking into my office.

I'm embarrassed, but Dez sticks her tongue out at Cordelia. I chuckle.

"Cordelia is happily married," I inform Dez. "Nothing has ever happened between us."

"And now nothing ever will," Dez assures.

"It's not like you to bring your relationships into the office," Cordelia comments, walking away. "I guess you want this one to make it past the first night."

Dez growls but stops when I kiss her cheek. I'm not sure why I did it, but it feels familiar, like I've been wasting time on strangers.

"Let's grab dinner," I say, standing straight.

"What do you have at the condo to cook?"

I look at her, confused that she actually thinks I cook.

"Nothing," I answer, helping her off the desk.

"So, what do you do for food?"

"You mean when I'm not at your parents' house?" I ask as we exit. "Pick up something from somewhere and go home.

Dez rolls her eyes. "There's a grocery store not far from your condo; let's stop there, and I'll make dinner."

"You know how to cook?" I ask, surprised as I lock the suite behind us.

"I cook at home quite often."

I laugh, and she playfully hits me. It hurts, just a little, again. I really need to get back in the gym.

"I've never seen you cook a day in my life."

"Well, that'll be another first for us," she says as we head to the parking garage.

"What was the first?" I innocuously ask.

"Valentine's Day."

"No way I was your first Valentine," I chuckle.

"You weren't," she says, walking ahead as we spot my SUV. "You were my first lover."

I stop walking. She doesn't notice at first, but after reaching the SUV and realizing I'm not there, she faces me.

"What's wrong?"

I can't even look into her eyes. "Dez, Valentine's Day was your first time having sex?" I whisper.

"Does your hearing diminish after turning thirty, or have you just listened to too many gavels being banged?" she asks, returning to me.

"Why are you acting like losing your virginity was no big deal?"

"It was a big deal. I enjoyed every moment of it," she says, wrapping her arms around me, "and the man I spent it with."

"It should've been romantic, with candles, music, flowers, and the man you love."

"I don't regret anything about our night, Justin," she says, releasing me. "Though I may not love you like a wife loves her husband," she lowers her head and whispers, "yet." She clears her throat and makes eye contact with me. "I do love you as a friend, and maybe, after a while, I can love you much more."

Why can't she read the gravity of her confession or of anything she's shared during the past three days? Or maybe I'm the one tripping. Maybe virginity and dating friends are too sentimental to me, so I have sex without attachment and refuse to date anyone. Dez is different, not because she's Romeo's sister, but because she's so confident about her decisions and feelings and... us. I want to know why; what does she see between us that I don't... yet?

"I haven't had a girlfriend in a long time," I whisper, wrapping my arms around her, "so please be patient with me."

She smiles before kissing my lips. "How does shrimp Alfredo sound for dinner?" she asks when she pulls away.

"It sounds great if you learned your mom's recipe."

She smirks. "I've mastered it."

Chapter 4: Justin

February 26, 2015

"I'm sorry I'm late, but let's go!" Dez says when I let her in my condo.

"I just got in myself. Court ran later than expected, and the traffic getting here was crazy," I say, walking back to my room. "Let me throw on something casual, and I'll be ready to go."

"How long is that going to take? If traffic is still bad, then we'll never make it on time. And then—"

"You look gorgeous," I say, cutting her off.

Dez is rarely on time for anything, so I'm not surprised. Her inability to arrive anywhere on time though, causes her to become anxious, and when she's anxious, she talks faster than an auctioneer. She does look gorgeous, though. She's wearing a pair of green, baggy cargo pants that stop right above her ankles. A plain nude shirt with mesh long sleeves decorated with roses and matching nude ankle boots finish her look. A green jacket is thrown over her arm, her hair is straightened with a side part, and she's wearing red lipstick.

"Thanks." She blushes.

"It won't take me long to change," I assure, unbuttoning my dress shirt. Within minutes, I'm in a long-sleeve, navy shirt with jeans and matching sneakers.

My phone vibrates while I'm brushing my hair in front of the dresser mirror. I'm surprised to see Dez's mom calling me. I reluctantly answer and put the call on speaker.

"Hey, Ms. Rose." I flip between calling her Ms. Rose and Ma since she has been a second mother to me since we met.

"Hey Justin. How have you been, sweetie?"

"I'm good. How are you doing?"

"I'm good, but I was wondering why you haven't been by lately."

Chuckling nervously, I put cocoa butter on my face and Vaseline on my lips. "It hasn't been that long, has it?"

"By the look of my pantry, it has been," she answers.

I give a genuine laugh as I head to the door. "I've been tied down with a few tasks on my end. I haven't been avoiding you... purposely," I say as Dez joins me.

"That's good because I want you to come over for dinner tonight."

I freeze, and Dez shakes her head while pointing to the time on her phone.

"I would love to, Ms. Rose, but I'm about to go on a date. Can I take a raincheck?"

"Why don't you bring your date over here? We have more than enough food, and we'd love to meet her."

Dez's anxious expression transforms into a mischievous smile. It's almost been two weeks since we started dating. She suggested we tell her family a while ago, but I refused. I want to tell everyone in an elegant manner—face to face, during Sunday brunch, perhaps when Romeo comes down for his court date next month. Dez wants to send a message to the family group chat.

"I don't think that's a good idea, Ms. Rose," I finally say.

"Justin, please." The desperation in her voice takes precedence over my boyish feelings. Something must be bothering her.

"I'm on my way," I say before hanging up.

Dez smacks her forehead and sighs. I escort her out, and as we silently descend in the elevator, I rack my brain trying to figure out what Ms. Rose needs. I'm already apprehensive about showing up with Dez, and having to worry about what is going on in Decatur creates more stress.

"When was the last time you spoke to Romeo?" I ask Dez as we head to the SUV.

She shrugs. "He never answers my calls and barely responds to my texts."

I nod while opening the passenger door for her. Romeo has been aloof with me too. I think the only reason he takes my calls is because I'm his lawyer. He only ever wants to talk about his case, and when I change the conversation to something like sports or working out, he ends the call. If he weren't my best friend, I would've stopped talking to him a long time ago.

"I wonder if that's what your mom wants to talk about," I say when I get in the driver's seat.

Dez studies my face before taking my hand in hers.

"What's going through your mind?" she asks.

"Aren't you nervous about showing up to your parents' house as a couple?"

"We're not asking for their permission," she states.

She's right, but as Georgia is a stand-your-ground state, her father doesn't need any permission to empty his handgun.

***

I unlock the front door and motion for Dez to walk in ahead of me.

"We're here," I say, locking the door.

Glancing around, I see that the Valentine's décor is still up. There are red felt hearts on the hallway walls, fake roses in the entryway vases, and a thick, sweet scent coming from the plug-ins.

"Hey, Jus," Ma says, approaching us. "You didn't have to cancel your date." She hugs me before hugging Dez.

"She probably backed out at the thought of having to meet us," Pop, Mr. Raymond, says, joining us. "It's not easy meeting a man's family."

"He didn't cancel his date," Dez informs. I glance at her, and she smiles, deviously.

"What are you doing here?" Pop asks Dez, kissing her cheek.

"I just flew into the neighborhood," Dez answers.

"You always get this dressed up when you fly into the neighborhood?" Pop asks as we make our way to the kitchen.

"I was about to go on a date. There's a movie about a woman and her neighbor that I've heard great reviews about."

Ma glances at me. "If your date didn't cancel, then where is she?"

I clear my throat, though nothing is stuck. If anything, I need some water for how parched I am. I've spoken in front of esteemed judges and represented millionaires and billionaires, but at this moment, I plead the fifth.

"Right here," Dez proudly announces. "I'm his date."

Ma glances at Pop. He grabs a pink and white striped plate from the cabinet and says, "Clearly, this is a one-time occurrence. You called him since you were both in the city and asked him to take you to the movies."

"Dezzy said date," Ma reminds, looking at Dez.

An awkward silence overcomes the kitchen. I go to the sink to wash my hands. Dez joins me at the sink, even handing me a paper towel. Taking a deep breath, I turn to face Ma and Pop, but Dez speaks before I open my mouth.

"Justin and I are dating."

Pop nearly drops his plate. He and Ma exchange an incomprehensible glance before looking at me and Dez. She takes two plates from the cabinet and hands me one.

"We've been dating since Valentine's Day," Dez continues, placing two pork chops on her plate. "We already had to pick a different movie time because Justin couldn't tell Mom no, so can we proceed with dinner so I can see this movie before it comes out on Blu-ray?"

To an outsider, Dez's remark sounds disrespectful, but she has been this candid for as long as I've known her. I assume her parents learned when she was being sassy, and when she wasn't. What I'm more interested in, however, is how comfortable she is about telling her parents about us.

"Let's eat," Ma says, getting a plate for herself.

Obviously, she and Pop have a lot of questions, but they utter not a single word. Once we all have a helping of pork chops, collard greens, and mac and cheese, we sit at the table. Pop stretches his hands out to say grace. I take one hand while Ma takes the other. Pop squeezes my hand, tightly, and begins praying.

"Amen," we all say before eating.

Ma and Pop continuously glance at one another, silently talking to each other. This is the quietest the table has ever been, making me uneasy.

"I invited you over to talk about Romeo," Ma finally announces. "We've called and texted him, but we rarely get a response from him. Since you're his best friend, we figured you would have some insight into what's going on with him."

Of course they're worried about him. We all are.

"As his lawyer, all I can tell you is that the case is progressing."

"And as his friend?" Pop asks.

I look at everyone around the table. I don't even speak to Dez about Romeo. Partly because I believe in keeping his business private since he's like my brother. Mostly because as cold as Dez acts, she loves Romeo with all her heart, and hearing the slightest negative thing about him would devastate her. She still doesn't know about the car accident he got into in college that landed him in the hospital for three days.

I sigh. "As his friend, Romeo is going through emotional hell. Jane won't even speak to him, and he's taking it very hard."

"My poor baby," Ma cries. "I don't want him in Brooklyn suffering alone. I'll visit him."

"That isn't a good idea," Dez and I say at the same time.

Ma looks at us.

"You're not someone who alleviates a situation," Dez explains. "You're emotionally high-strung, and you rub off on everyone around you. Romeo needs someone grounded; that's not you."

"Fine, but I don't want to sit here and do nothing."

"He'll be in town in a few weeks... to settle business," I say, trying to be as discreet as possible.

Ma and Pop nod their heads.

"We can wait until he gets here to love on him physically," Ma says, finding some solace.

"Until then, let's send him a care package and uplifting texts," Pop suggests.

The rest of us nod, and we continue eating. Dinner isn't silent anymore, which is soothing.

"We may still be able to catch a showing at Eastside Theatre," Dez suggests as we put our plates and forks in the dishwasher.

I forgot all about Eastside Theatre; they recently opened.

"I'm down. I'll buy tickets on my phone," I say, reaching into my pocket.

"Let me grab some outfits from my room, and I'll be ready," she says, closing the dishwasher and dashing out of the kitchen.

I walk to the foyer while purchasing tickets for the 9:55 PM showing of the movie.

"Justin," Pop says, catching me off guard. "I appreciate you coming over on such short notice."

"Anything for you and Ma," I say, dropping my phone in my pocket.

"I know, that's why we're going to have a brief conversation about you and Dezzy before having a longer one Saturday afternoon. Alone."

I clear my throat. If Dez is going to be forthright with them, then so will I. "Sure, Pop. What's up?"

"How exactly did you two start dating?" Ma asks.

"We ran into each other on Valentine's Day, went to dinner, and had a good time. Two days later we decided to become a couple." Though I'm being honest, Dez's parents don't need to know how we ended our first date.

"Is that why you've been avoiding us?" Ma asks.

I chuckle, feeling silly. "Yes, ma'am. I didn't know how everyone would react. I wanted to tell y'all, but I didn't know how, so I ended up isolating myself from you guys."

"How does Romeo feel about it?" Pop asks.

I shrug. "Romeo has no idea that Dez and I are dating. All he wants to talk about is his divorce and Jane. Any time I change the conversation even slightly, he's finished talking and hangs up."

Ma and Pop look at each other before looking at me.

"Justin, you and Desdemona are two consenting adults. It's not like you're her first boyfriend, but it is shocking to see you two together. Nonetheless, you don't have to stay away from here because y'all are dating. You've been like a son to us for the last twelve years, and nothing will change that, so don't feel the need to be distant," Ma says.

"Thanks," I say before looking at Pop.

"What are you waiting on me to say?" he asks.

I shrug. "Anything."

"There's not much to say. Y'all have only been together for two weeks, so I'm not giving you the 'take care of my daughter and don't hurt her' speech. But I will leave you with two words of advice. First, I hope being with Dezzy means you've left your womanizing ways in the past because second, regardless of how things go between you two, we are still a family. Y'all can't be ugly to each other if y'all ever break up because, like Rose said, we've been a family for the last twelve years. We can't have you two breaking that up. Aside from that," Pop stretches his hand to me, "date with my blessing."

"Thanks." I shake his hand.

"We don't need your blessing," Dez says, popping up. "But I know it means a lot to Justin."

Ma folds her arms and glares at Dez. Dez grimaces before giving her father a hug.

"The last two weeks have been great, you guys. Stop worrying."

I look at Dez and smile. The last two weeks have been great, and I'm still eager to see what the future holds.

I take the bag that she's packed and motion for her to head out the door. Pop didn't have to instruct me to take care of Dez because that's something I effortlessly do. I haven't spoken to another woman romantically since Valentine's Day, so there is no need to worry about me hurting her. Dez kisses my cheek before walking out. Ma smiles at me, and I blush. Dez and I are going to have to figure out our relationship, but I'm sure we'll be just fine.

Chapter 5: Dezzy

March 12, 2015

"I'm circling back around. I'll see you in a few minutes," Justin tells Romeo.

Romeo hangs up without saying anything else.

"He doesn't sound like he's too happy," I note as Justin follows the airport loop around to arrivals.

"Well, he is here to finalize the divorce he thought was finalized in January," Jus reminds.

"I know, but I thought he'd be a little happier since he's at the finish line."

"Unless Jane is on the other side, I really don't think he cares," Justin whispers.

I glance at him. He's been making sly remarks like that whenever I inquire about Romeo. I can discern Justin isn't telling me everything, but I don't want to put him in a situation where he'll have to choose me or Romeo. Mostly because I fear he'll choose his best friend over me in a heartbeat.

"There he is," I say, pointing at my brother. He's wearing a matching gray GSU hoodie and sweatpants set. He looks shabby, for lack of a better word. His hair is past due for a lineup, and his facial hair looks like it hasn't been tended to in weeks. His eyelids are baggy, and his eyes look weary. In short, he's aged since January.

Romeo walks to the car, mindlessly. He opens the passenger door, where I am, and gives me a dumbfounded look.

"What're you—" He closes the door before finishing his sentence. I hadn't even thought about sitting in the back. That's where I usually sat whenever the three of us rode together.

Turning around, I smile at Romeo and playfully hit his leg. "Justin was nice enough to give me a ride to Decatur since we're not that far from each other. You know I have to see my big bro whenever he comes home."

"New York is home," he mumbles, moving away from me.

I face forward in my seat, and Justin glances at me before looking at Romeo in the rearview mirror.

"You look like you've been through the wringer. How about we grab some drinks before heading to your parents' house?" Justin suggests.

"You'd look like this too if you'd been through hell. Let's just go to Decatur," Romeo dryly responds.

Justin and I look at each other before I turn on the radio. We don't say anything the rest of the ride, and Romeo preoccupies himself on his phone. I can't believe that the downcast zombie in the backseat is the once vibrant and cheery man that was here two months ago.

***

Romeo hops out of the car as soon as we pull into the driveway. I remain seated as Justin makes his way to me and opens my door.

"Tonight, should be interesting," he whispers as we follow Romeo to the front door.

Mom hugs and kisses Romeo as we enter. He stands there, not even doing as much as putting an arm around her. Dad looks at me and Justin as Romeo makes his way to the kitchen for dinner. We both shake our heads.

We offered to pick Romeo up so that we could tell him about our relationship. Romeo's mood, however, deterred either of us from mentioning it.

"You couldn't have gotten a haircut before you left New York?" Dad asks
as we fix our plates.

"Leave him alone, Gary," Mom orders.

"He's appearing in court tomorrow. The least he could've gotten is a
shape-up," Dad counters.

Rome silently places beefaroni on his plate before sitting at the table.
Mom has decorated it, as well as the rest of the house, in green and floral
arrangements.

"Where's Donna?" Dad asks. Justin and I glare at him.

"I don't know. I bought her and her kid a one-way ticket, and they
should've landed earlier today."

"Since we're getting straight to the point, would you tell us the reason
why the divorce wasn't finalized? Justin hardly speaks about it," Mom says
as the rest of us sit.

Romeo gives Justin a surprised look. It's the most emotion he's shown
all night.

"Donna says the kid is mine, and the divorce won't be finalized until
paternity is determined."

"That should be open and shut," Mom says, relaxing.

Justin and Romeo glance at each other but say nothing.

"And how does Jane feel about this?" Dad asks.

Romeo doesn't answer. Either he didn't hear, or he doesn't care to
respond. Justin clears his throat.

"A congresswoman invited me to a dinner party next weekend. I hope
to become acquainted with some DA's and criminal attorneys since I'm
thinking about going into that field."

Mom picks up on Justin's change of conversation and follows up with
some questions. I'm too disheartened to participate, though.

"Would you like some lemonade?" Mom offers Romeo. "It's homemade, since that's the only kind of juice you drink now."

"Mom!" I scold.

When Jane and Romeo visited, she proudly announced that she's been personally making him juice since they've started dating.

"Lemonade sounds great. Thanks, Mom," Romeo says, getting up. He pours himself a glass, drinks it, and then puts his dishes in the sink. I want to ask him to play some video games together as a way to distract him, but he walks down the hallway instead of coming back to the table.

"I didn't mean to upset him," Mom says, sadly.

"You didn't upset him. Jane is still a sore subject," Justin states before drinking some lemonade.

"She still won't talk to him?" Dad asks.

Justin raises his eyes above his glass, like a deer caught in headlights.

"Is that a yes?" I ask, concerned.

Justin places his cup down. "I'm sharing this as family, not his lawyer," he says, making eye contact with each of us. "Jane broke up with him."

"What?" my parents and I ask in unison.

"Romeo was hosting Jane at his house for dinner when Donna arrived and announced that they were still married and the child is Romeo's. Jane hasn't spoken to him since, and he still isn't over it."

"Jane is being overdramatic," I say. I didn't really speak to her when she visited, but I could tell that she didn't play any games.

"Overdramatic?" Jus asks me. "You would react the same way she did."

"So now you're siding with some broad over your best friend?" I ask.

"I'm not siding with her. Y'all know I'll have Romeo's back 'til the day I die, but that doesn't mean I don't see things from Jane's perspective. She does not want to be with a married man, and that's pretty common for people in her position."

"Did she genuinely have no idea that he was still married?" Dad asks.

"Even we thought the divorce was final, dear," Mom chimes in.

"I always told my son that he has to be completely honest when he's in a relationship. Now he wants to mope around because his actions led to such drastic consequences?"

"I agree with Dezzy," Mom shares. "Jane overreacted a bit. It's not like Romeo was actively seeing Donna, or the kid is actually his."

Justin brings the last spoonful of beefaroni to his mouth.

"Right, Justin?" Mom insists.

Justin clears his throat. "Just because Donna was unfaithful to Romeo doesn't mean he was unfaithful to her. There's definitely a chance that Romeo is the father."

"He better not be," Dad says, upset. "We finally got rid of Donna, and I refuse to have her worm her way back into this family. I never wanted Romeo to marry her."

"We're past that, Gary," Mom says. "None of us wanted Romeo to marry her, but it still happened."

"Right, but I feel like Romeo is in his room, depressed because Justin half-assed this case since Romeo is his friend."

"Whoa," Justin interjects. "I didn't half-ass anything. I wasn't in the bed with him and Donna at any point in their marriage. I don't know what they did or when they did it."

"You're supposed to be the best divorce lawyer in Atlanta, but you couldn't make sure that your best friend's case is taken care of?"

"I did not drop the ball here, Pop," Justin says, his volume increasing. "I did everything I was supposed to do. Donna and her lawyer started playing games when she began alleging that the child is Romeo's. I know you're looking for a scapegoat, but I'd appreciate it if you find someone else." Justin pushes out his chair and stands up. "All I'm finna do is what I always do: work my ass off representing him tomorrow to make sure he'll no longer be married to her. If it's the kid you're worried about, then you better get to praying 'cause I can't defend against genetics." Justin drops his dishes in the sink and walks out the front door.

"You know Justin would never sabotage Romeo," Mom says. "What's happening isn't Justin's fault. You should apologize."

"Whatever," Dad grumbles before dumping his dishes and leaving.

Mom shakes her head and walks to the sink. My heart aches as I help her load the dishwasher. I'm torn between being by Justin's side and trying to comfort Romeo. Is this Justin's fault to some extent, or is it entirely Romeo's fault for not being honest? I'm always honest, no matter who or what the situation is. Obviously, I inherited this quality from Dad. Romeo is more like Mom, sugarcoating everything, assuming it'll ease life's tensions. The only thing I've ever held back in life was my feelings for Justin, and even those seeped out eventually.

Once the kitchen is clean and the dishwasher is running, I go to my room and change into a large, white t-shirt and green boy shorts. I had no idea Romeo was going through all of this alone. I'm heartbroken for him. He told me about Jane after their first date last November, and I discerned he really loved her when he brought her home in January. He must be devastated that she broke up with him over something so trivial. I wish there was a way to console him, but it's clear he doesn't want to be healed by anyone other than her.

I hear the front door open and close before hearing a door down the hall open. Cracking my door, I see Justin leaving the guest room and heading to Romeo's.

"Jus," I softly call.

He looks at me and walks to my door.

"What's up, Dez?" He asks, looking into my eyes.

"Can you sleep in here tonight?" I whisper. We've only shared a bed once since Valentine's Day.

"Your parents' room is right there," he says, looking at it. "There's no way I can—"

"Please?" I ask, a tear escaping my eye.

His eyes widen before he pushes himself into my room and closes the door. He sits on the armchair and pulls me onto his lap.

"Are you really that upset about Romeo?" Justin asks, caressing my face.
I nod before burying my face in his chest.

"I can't stand seeing him like this. There's never anything I can do but look on. He's my brother; he's been there for me for everything. Why can't I do anything to ease his pain?" His shirt muffles my cries while he rubs my back. "That idiot," I say, catching my breath.

"Why does he have to love so hard?"

"Can we truly help how hard we fall for someone?" Justin asks, his voice deep and heavy. "You really only have two options, don't you? Keep your guard up and remain single, or be vulnerable, even if that means giving someone the ammunition to break your heart. The extremity depends on the individual."

I raise my head a little to look at him.

"The heart is a deceitful thing, Dez," he says before kissing my cheek.

I take his face in mine before kissing his lips. He wraps his arms around me tighter as I feel his heartbeat increase.

I go under his shirt and wrap my arms around his torso.

"Dez," he whispers, biting my bottom lip. "We can't do this. Not right now and definitely not here."

"But you're ready," I say, straddling him. He lets out a low moan.

"Sex makes relationships hazy. We've hardly been together for a month. Let's continue exploring—"

"I'm trying to explore you," I say, kissing him.

"You just want to feel better, but this isn't the way."

"Why does it matter how I feel better, as long as it happens?"

"Because then you may associate sex with only being a pain reliever, instead of an intimate, breath-snatching, out-of-body experience with the one you love."

I'm sure my mouth is drooling. Valentine's night was magical, but I didn't realize it could get better than that. He chuckles.

"I promise I won't associate it with only being a pain reliever. Come on,"

I say, wrapping my legs around him.

"No."

"Please," I beg, looking into his eyes.

He picks me up and lays me on the bed a few feet away. "You can't get whatever you want just because you say please," he says, seriously.

"I know," I whisper.

He takes off his shirt and pants before lying on top of me. "So, we're not having sex. We're at your parents' house, and I don't have any condoms."

I pout, and he smiles.

"You really are spoiled," he says, slipping his hands under my t-shirt.

He nibbles at my neck while caressing my breasts. He kisses my lips and arms before lifting my shirt. He continues kissing my body, biting and licking places like my inner thigh, eliciting soft moans from me. His hands and lips all over me almost feel like the real thing, but it's pleasurable enough to bring me ecstasy. When I push him away because I'm unable to take anymore, he smiles, conceitedly. I roll my eyes and get under the covers.

"Goodnight," I aggressively say, pulling the covers over my head.

He joins me a few moments later. He wraps his arms around my waist and says, "Goodnight, Dez," before kissing my cheek.

Chapter 6: Dezzy

March 21, 2015

"I just feel uneasy about hanging out with a bunch of your friends," Justin admits as we pull up to my friend's townhouse in Marietta.

"I felt uneasy attending that congresswoman's dinner party with you a few days ago, but I gave it my best. All I'm asking for you to do is give it a try. If you're not having a good time within an hour, then we'll leave," I bargain.

"Fine," he says, unbuckling his seatbelt. "I'll give it a shot."

I turn the knob when we get to the front door and walk in.

"Breaking and entering is a crime," Justin jokes.

I hit him playfully while closing the door behind us.

"Nancy!" I call, walking to the living room at the back of the house. "We're here."

"Dezzy!" Nancy cheers, stopping me in the hallway so we can hug. "I'm so glad you're here."

"Girl, I told you I was coming," I say, letting her go. "And this is my boyfriend, Justin." Those words still feel foreign rolling off my tongue.

"Nice to meet you," Nancy says, shaking Justin's hand. "I can see why Dezzy's been too busy to hang with us lately."

"Shut up," I say, blushing. "Where's Alex?" I ask as we make it to the living room.

"I'm on kitchen duty, unfortunately," he calls through the kitchen peep-hole.

"Alex and Nancy are married," I explain to Justin. "Nancy was one of my suitemates in college."

"Dezzy!" Cindy says, jumping off the couch. "It's about time you got here. Now it's really a party."

"Then turn on some music and let's get it started!" I say, hugging her.

She glances behind me. "You really brought Justin instead of Romeo?" she asks, disappointed.

Justin glances from Cindy to me. "Have we met?"

Cindy and I give Justin a perplexed look.

"She and I have been best friends since I moved to Decatur. You've seen her at the house plenty of times. "You've even given us rides around the city," I remind. Not to mention, Cindy's the only person I've confessed my feelings about Justin to.

Justin squints his eyes before shrugging. "Hey," he dryly greets.

Cindy rolls her eyes. "I wish you would've brought your gorgeous broth-er, Romeo."

"Didn't you come here with a date?" I inquire. "Where is he?"

Cindy rolls her eyes. "He's in the bathroom. What a lame. Online dating is overrated."

"Food is finished. Let's eat and get started with our game night," Nancy orders.

Shortly after drinks and dinner, Nancy turns on the game and puts in *Let's Dance.*

"Do you dance, Justin?" she asks.

"A little," he replies.

I look at him, surprised. "A little? I've never seen you dance."

"There's a lot you've never seen me do," he teases.

"Well, put your moves where your mouth is," Cindy challenges, handing him a controller.

Justin gets up and does a solo dance to Michael Jackson's "Chicago." He smoothly glides across the floor, moving his arms effortlessly. Everyone cheers as he beats Alex's high score. I stare, amazed. Is there anything this man can't do?

"Dance with me, Dez," he orders, tossing a controller my way.

"I'm not all that good at *Let's Dance,*" I admit.

"I got you," Jus assures, stretching his hand to me.

"We'll play too," Nancy says, grabbing a controller for herself and Alex.

I pick up the controller and stand beside Justin as he chooses "Uptown Funk."

I start off by copying Justin before looking on the screen and following the on-screen avatar. I'm impressed to snag third place.

"Need a break already?" I tease Justin when he downs some punch.

"Just giving someone else the opportunity to play. I have great stamina."

I raise an eyebrow. We only went one round Valentine's night; was he holding back for my sake?

"I'm tapped out for the night," Nancy says, rubbing her stomach. She's barely begun to show, but the first trimester has already taken a toll on her.

"Let's do one together, Dez," Justin says, choosing "[I've Had] The Time of My Life."

"Here you go with songs no one knows," I say, standing up.

"That song is a classic," Cindy declares. "Did you not see the movie?"

"There's a movie?" I ask, rolling my eyes.

"We can watch the movie later," Justin says, as the song starts.

He saunters over to me so suavely that I miss my cue to come in.

"Pay up," he instructs, smiling.

I try my best to follow the moves on the screen. While I may be good at dancing freely, following directions has always been my drawback. The dance is intimate, with Justin grabbing my waist at certain moments and holding my hand at others. The moves are repetitive, thankfully, and I'm able to enjoy dancing with Justin.

"That was something," I say, catching my breath as the song fades out.

"It's not over yet," he tells me. "You have to run toward me and jump into my arms."

"What?" I yell.

"Just do it," Justin demands.

I do as told, and he not only catches me but also lifts me over his head. I can't help but laugh as he spins me around.

"Enough, you two; let's play something else," Cindy complains.

Justin lets me down slowly, and we take a seat at the dining table with everyone else.

"Let's play Buzz Words," Alex suggests, shuffling the cards. "Couple versus couple. Guys, give the clues first, and you ladies have to guess the word based on the clues we give."

"We're not going to win," Cindy whines.

"We aren't either," I agree.

"Don't be so sure," Justin says.

"They're married. "They know everything about each other," I remind them.

Justin shakes his head and eats some chips while looking over Alex's shoulder to make sure he didn't say any words he wasn't supposed to. Alex and Nancy impressively score fourteen out of nineteen.

"We're next," Jus says, grabbing a stack of cards. "We got this, Dez," he encourages, smiling at me.

I nod, finding his confidence admirable.

"Our college mascot," Justin starts.

"Panther."

"The extracurricular activity you did in ninth grade and wanted to quit because you didn't have what it takes."

"Marching band," I say, rolling my eyes.

"The shade of the dress you wore to your junior prom."

I stare at him, speechless. He only saw me a few minutes before my date, and I walked out the door. There are very few pictures of me from junior prom because most of them were with the date that I no longer speak to.

"You remember her dress color, but you don't remember me?" Cindy scoffs.

"We're skipping," Justin says, about to change the card.

"No. Lavender," I finally answer.

"The meaning of your middle name."

"Flower."

"You tried out for this but didn't make it."

"Step team."

Justin spouts clue after clue, tailoring each card to me until the timer goes off. I'm in awe; I can't believe he remembers so much about me.

"We got twenty for twenty," he says, stretching his hand to me for a high-five. I give him a weak one, still overwhelmed.

Cindy and her date go next, and they get about half of the cards. When it's my turn to give clues to Justin, I try to take his approach, but I quickly realize I don't know as much about him as he does about me. I'm stuck giving him clues about my life.

"I did this my first two years of college."

"Cheer."

"Romeo was a blank chair in college."

"Second."

"The award-winning book series I was obsessed with."

"*Agent Chris?*" he guesses.

I nod. We don't get as many points as when Justin gave the clues, but we still end up with the most points overall. We play a game of Phase 10 before deciding to call it a night.

"Justin really knows you," Cindy comments as we help Nancy with the dishes.

"He does, doesn't he?" I ask as he and Alex return from dumping the trash outside.

"You're right, Dez. I did have a great time tonight."

"It's great to hear you admit that I'm right," I smirk.

"You ready to go?" he asks, rubbing my back while looking into my eyes. Nancy and Cindy sigh dreamily.

"Don't forget to invite us to the wedding," Nancy says.

Justin chuckles while facing them. "Whose wedding?"

I look at him skeptically.

"Your wedding with Dezzy, of course," Cindy says, gathering her belongings. "Unless you don't plan on getting married."

"All my years of being a divorce lawyer have taught me one thing: marriage is the end of all good relationships."

"Don't say that," Alex says. "Nancy and I just celebrated two years."

"You don't truly believe that do you?" I ask Justin.

"Of course I do. I've seen people file for divorce over the most mundane reasons: 'He snores too loud,' 'She wears perfume I don't like,' 'She can't cook,' 'He doesn't make enough money.' Then there are the more extreme ones:' I fell in love with their sibling,' 'They gained twenty pounds,' 'They had an outside baby.' All of those cases just taught me that marriage ruins everything because I'm convinced that all of those people were happier when they were dating."

"That's a bleak look on life, man," Alex says. "Every marriage doesn't end in divorce."

"Watch what you say; you're messing with my paycheck," Justin says before everyone except me laughs. He looks at me then. "You ready?"

Nodding, I grab my purse and walk to the front door.

***

"You've been silent this whole ride," Justin notes, parking at his condo.

"Have I?" *I couldn't tell with how loud my thoughts were the entire drive.*

"You sound upset. What's wrong?" he asks, killing the engine and taking off his seatbelt.

I get out of the car without saying anything. He doesn't seem bothered that I didn't wait for him to open the door for me. I still haven't answered his question by the time we make it on the elevator.

"Dez," he says as we ride to his floor.

"When were you going to tell me that you never wanted to get married?"

"What?" he asks, taken aback as we step off the elevator.

"What do you mean 'what'?" I ask, fuming. "Amid laughing and cracking jokes, you confessed to all my friends that you'll never get married."

"I don't want to get married," he repeats, unlocking his door.

"Why didn't you ever tell me that?"

"It's not like you want to get married," he scoffs, walking into the living room. "C'mon, Dez, you actually want to get married?"

"Of course I want to get married!" I yell, following him. "You think I want to spend my entire life dating a guy just to be recognized in his obituary as his 'special friend?'"

Justin stares at me, flabbergasted.

"Say something," I demand.

"I don't know what to say, Dez."

I exhale deeply while rubbing my temples with my right hand.

"Don't say anything then," I say, walking into the hallway. "I'm leaving."

"It's after one in the morning, Dez. I'm not letting you leave this late. Where would you even go?"

"I'm going back to campus," I say, unlocking the front door.

"At least let me give you a ride, and we can talk about this in the morning," he says, stopping me from turning the knob.

"No. I don't want anything from you. "I don't want any rides or any phone calls or anything," I say as hot tears stream down my face. "If the last month has been nothing but a joke to you, or if you're dating me because

I'm a placeholder in your life, then I'm leaving. I'm not finna waste your time, and I'm not finna let you waste mine."

"No one's wasting anyone's time," he insists.

"Get out of my way."

"I'm not letting you walk to campus. At least let me call a cab."

"You don't have to *let* me do anything; I'll do what I want to 'cause you obviously don't care about me. Have you just been indulging me until you found a new toy to play with?" I ask, my voice breaking. "We never even had to take things this far. I would've been content just wondering what we could've been as find the man I'm supposed to be with."

Justin takes me by my shoulders and pulls me to him. He uses one hand to lift my chin so we can stare into each other's eyes.

"Desdemona," he says. I'm surprised he even remembers my real name. "I want to be with you."

"What?" I weakly ask.

"I don't want our relationship to end. You're not a placeholder in my life. You never told me you dreamed of getting married one day."

"I didn't think I had to," I whisper.

"Of course you have to. If we could read each other's minds, then you would've known that marriage is the furthest thing from mine."

"But why is it? How could you know everything about me, from the color of my first prom dress to the meaning of my middle name, but say you don't want to get married?" He's rejecting the concept of marriage, but it feels like he's rejecting me. "There are married people who love each other and won't bat an eye at someone else. You have to know that all marriages don't end in divorce."

"Do I?"

"Look at my parents. Look at your parents. Happy and long-lasting marriages exist."

"I guess you're right," he whispers, breaking eye contact.

"I'm not finna date you for the rest of my life, Justin. I'm not giving you an ultimatum, but I'd rather us end things now and return to being friends if we're never going to make it to the altar. I'm not saying I want to wake up and marry you tomorrow. I don't know when, if ever, it'll happen. I've been enjoying our relationship, and I wouldn't be opposed to us being married, but I'm also not going to stay with you and waste my time," I say before turning his head to mine. "I'm not expecting your feelings about marriage to change overnight; in fact, they may never change. But I need you to know that mine aren't going to change either."

"So where does that leave us?" he asks, wiping my tears.

"I don't know."

Chapter 7: Justin

April 2, 2015

"You 'bout ready to go?" I ask Cordelia while walking into the reception area.

She glances at the crystal, octagon clock hanging above the exit.

"It's three seconds past four. Where are you in a rush to go?" she inquires.

"I'm going to see Dez."

Cordelia raises an eyebrow. "So, she did make it past the first date. Don't tell me you've finally allowed a woman to snag you."

"She's not some woman. She's... how long before you're ready to lock up?" I ask, not wanting to explain myself. Cordelia chuckles and begins closing the folders on her desk.

"My husband is picking me up tonight, so I'll get him to assist with closing duties."

"Great," I say, darting out the door and locking it behind me. I don't ever leave Cordelia to close up alone unless it's one of the times her husband stops by. He usually does it when they're going on a date after work. I unlock the suite door and poke my head inside.

"Today isn't your anniversary, is it?"

She laughs. "No. I just have some exciting news to share with him."

"Okay," I say, relieved I didn't miss it again. "I won't be in tomorrow...

hopefully."

"I know, Mr. Campbell. Would you get out of here? Dez is waiting on you."

Nodding, I lock the suite door again and leave.

Dez and I have barely spoken since the couple's game night. We've only seen each other once in that time. I haven't entertained another woman in this time, though a lot of old flames have hit my line. I don't ever want to make Dez cry like that again, nor do I want her to think what we have is temporary. Interestingly, the last week and half without her have left me feeling empty; like a piece of me is missing. She was on Spring Break this week, and worked every shift she could, rather than using a day off to spend time together. Dez was so happy during the game night. I surprised myself with how much I remembered about her, but I'm the type of person who pays attention to the small details of those closest to me. I would've known as much about Romeo too if he and I were playing.

Stopping at a nearby convenience store, I run in and head straight to the bakery section. I grab the last box of chocolate covered donut holes, leave a ten on the counter, and get back in my illegally parked car. I don't even know what shift Dez is working today, but instincts tell me she's there. Thankfully, I find a parking space down the street from Groove's.

I grab the donuts and walk in.

"Table for one?" the hostess asks, grabbing a menu. I glance around the partially full restaurant.

"Is Dezzy here?" The name feels foreign rolling off my tongue.

The hostess looks at me hesitantly before going into the kitchen. She and Dez emerge a few seconds later.

"Justin?" Dez asks, approaching me. "What are you doing here?" Her hair is straightened and parted down the middle. She's wearing her usual uniform, a long-sleeve button down black shirt, sneakers, and a skirt. It makes me wonder if she wears a skirt to work every day, and if so, how many heads does she turn?

"Can we talk?"

Dez glances at her watch. "I have some time left in my break. Sure," she agrees, leading me to a table.

I thank the hostess before following Dez.

"What's up?" she asks, sitting at a booth.

I sit across from her.

"I miss you," I blurt out.

She's taken aback, and I slide the donuts across the table to her.

Smiling, she opens the box. "I guess you felt the distance between us too. People usually say that distance is good."

"A break is good, sure. But space forces you to adapt without that person, and when they return, you realize you don't need them the way you once did."

Dez looks into my eyes then. "I've missed you too," she admits.

"It's almost been two weeks since I've had a home cooked meal," I joke.

Laughing, she pops a donut into her mouth. "And I bet you've been eating a lot of junk food," she teases.

I smile. "What do you have planned for this weekend?"

"Nothing. I'm free Friday through Monday."

"Let's go away," I offer.

Her eyes light up. "All four days?"

I shrug. "I have a meeting on Monday, but I can attend over the phone."

"Where are we going?"

"Savannah, unless you—"

"Savannah sounds great!" she squeals. "I've been yearning for some water. You'll come swimming with me, right? We'll..."

There she goes speaking faster than Foghorn Leghorn again.

"I'll take care of everything," I say, cutting her off.

She smiles at me then. "I get off at ten."

"I'll be parked outside."

"I have to go home to pack though."

"I can take you."

"I don't want to wake my parents up by coming in that late." She smirks before eating another donut. "Guess I'll have to come back to your place."

Chuckling, I shake my head. I've never been a quitter; I've always been one to see things to the finish line. My ideals about marriage haven't changed in the past few days, but I'm determined to see how far Dez, and I will go. I haven't had a girlfriend since high school, and I've forgotten how comforting it is to be with the same person.

April 3, 2015

"Okay, let's play one more."

"Another game, Dez?" I sigh.

"It's the last one, I promise. We still have an hour to go, and I'm trying to make sure you don't fall asleep."

It's ten in the morning, so I'm nowhere close to tired. "If you're worried about me falling asleep, then why don't you drive?"

"Yeah, right! I'm on Spring Break."

Chuckling, I shake my head. Ms. Rose is the road trip extraordinaire, mapping out sites to see, the best exits to take breaks at, and the best local restaurants to dine in. She also creates engaging road trip games, including the one Dez and I just concluded, the License Plate game. Dez obviously picked this up from her mother. Not only did she create an itinerary for us, but she packed what she refers to as "the essentials." Towels, blankets, beach chairs, sunscreen and bug spray—everything I probably would've bought after we arrived in Savannah.

"What's the game, Dez?"

"Well, it's not really a game. It's a deck of cards with open-ended questions for couples to discuss."

"Those are lame and boring."

"Are not!" she argues.

"They repeat the same questions, making me feel like I'm on trial."

"They'll help us connect and know each other better. Let's just do a few."

"Since when do you need a card game to ask me something?"

"I don't always know the right things to ask you. For example," she draws a card, "do you have any tattoos?"

"You know I don't."

"But I don't know why."

I glance at her. "I'm scared of needles." She bursts out laughing, and I shake my head. "I'm done playing."

"No, wait," she says, gasping for air, "I'm not laughing at your fear. Justin, you're in your 30s; there's no way you're still terrified of a little prick."

"We aren't talking about flu shots, Dez. We're talking about being repeatedly stabbed in a specific area until a design is carved onto a given body part."

Dez faces me, a smirk on her lips. "Do you even get flu vaccines?"

"They offer vaccines via nasal spray nowadays."

Dez doubles over laughing, and I roll my eyes.

"This game is stupid."

"No, I'll behave," she says, wiping tears from her eyes. "While this is a judgement free zone, it's not a laugh free one. You know I have a tattoo, so I'll go to the next question," she says before drawing again. "What's your best childhood memory?"

I think for a moment. My childhood was great, so choosing just one memory is difficult. Should I tell her about going cherry and apple picking? My first time at a pumpkin patch? Then I chuckle.

"When I was twelve, my cousins and I went joyriding on my dad's tractor."

"What?" she asks, surprised.

"My cousins were visiting for a week. We decided to pull an all-nighter, so we drank all the soda we could find, ate loads of sugary foods, and stayed up watching VHS tapes. Unfortunately, we fell asleep within a matter of hours." I chuckle while shaking my head.

"My eldest cousin, Sabrina, woke us up around one in the morning, and we were all disappointed about our inability to stay up. But then she had an idea—let's go for a ride in the tractor."

"It only has two seats at most," Dez says.

"Give me time to paint the picture. We sneak out the house and into the barn without a hitch. The tractor roared to life, and we were on our way. Through the doors and across the field to the driveway. 'Where are we going?' I asked Sabrina. 'I dunno. Let's see what's happenin' in town.' So off we went, she and I seated inside, and her two younger brothers holding onto the sides. A few minutes later, I see my dad's pickup truck trailing us. My mom is yelling out the window with rollers in her head while Dad is honking his horn. Sabrina told me to speed up," I say, laughing. "So, I let out a war cry at the top of my lungs and floor it, and we take off going a whippin' 30 miles an hour. My cousins are holding onto the sides for dear life, and I'm runnin' off pure adrenaline. My dad speeds up and blocks the intersection. I hit the brakes, one of my cousins fell off."

Dez chuckles before asking, "What happened next?"

I shrug. "I think my cousin only had a few minor bruises, but my parents were livid. They worked us like farmhands for the rest of the week. We woke up at 5AM, had to get the eggs, clean the chicken coop, and milk the cows and goats. We've done those chores before, but when we wanted, not at the crack of dawn."

Dez smiles then. "You don't talk about your life in Missouri much."

"There's not much to share."

She rolls her eyes. "You lived there for eighteen years, and you want me to believe that there's not much to share? Your eyes lit up as you told that story."

"They did not."

"How would you know?" she challenges. "Your accent even came out, country boy."

I shake my head. "I was born there, but I'm from Atlanta, just like you."

"Boy, I'm from Brooklyn!" We make eye contact before bursting out laughing.

She's no more from Brooklyn than I'm from Atlanta, but we obviously feel the same way about our hometowns.

"What's your favorite childhood memory?" I ask her.

"Romeo and I went to spend the summer in Brooklyn with our grand-parents one year. I was still in elementary school, maybe fifth grade. We spent the entire day at Coney Island. We got Nathan's hotdogs, cotton candy, and snow cones. We walked the boardwalk, played in the water, and eventually got on the rollercoasters. I was terrified of any rollercoaster that did more than spin riders in a circle, but I wanted to keep hanging out with my big bro, so I went on every ride he did. He eventually noticed my apprehension because he held my hand. It was comforting and distracted me from the butterflies in my stomach during the drops and loops. We had a great time."

"That's sweet. Much safer than I would've expected from you, but sweet."

"Whatever. The next question is —"

"The last question you mean."

"Fine. The last question is what was your longest relationship, and why did it end?"

My chest tightens. I hadn't thought about that, let alone *her*, in quite some time. "You answer first."

Dez props her head on her hand as she thinks. "Sophomore year of college I began dating this guy named Rick. We had a good thing going for a while, but as much as I wanted it to last, I knew it wouldn't."

I don't recall Dez bringing home any boyfriends, let alone someone she dated for a whole year. "Why wouldn't it last?"

"We had two different ways of thinking. The biggest difference being that he believed in not telling me things because he thought protecting my feelings was better than telling me the truth, and I believe in telling the truth no matter what. He wasn't cheating, to my knowledge, but just the fact of being deceptive or not honest enough because of how you think I'll react shows a lack of trust. It also made me feel like a kid, as if my emotions and reactions were in the palm of his hands."

She's right, that would never work for her. She's too free-spirited for that.

"So, I broke up with him after Spring Break. He was pissed and accused me of making the greatest mistake of my life."

"And how do you feel years later?" I ask.

She chuckles. "I have yet to make the greatest mistake of my life. I would never marry a jerk like him."

"So, you've always known you wanted to get married?"

"Since I was a kid."

"Then why didn't you wait until you were married to have sex?" I ask.

She looks at me. "Why didn't you?"

"Because I don't want to get married... I mean, I did at one point, but once I realized it would never happen, sex was just something to do."

"What made you change your mind about getting married?"

"Why didn't you wait?" I repeat.

"Because you're someone I trust, and someone I've wanted to be with for a long time. What changed your mind about marriage?"

I exhale. "I don't like talking about Alana, so please don't bring her back up after I tell you about her."

"Okay."

"Alana and I started dating during sophomore year of high school. We were what the school considered a power couple: good grades, liked by everyone, and in a handful of extracurriculars. We were tight, our parents were tight, and I just knew our relationship would last forever. During senior year, we planned our post-high school plans. Being a lawyer was always my goal, and she wanted to study psychology. We applied to the same schools and mapped out our entire lives. Her family loved me and mine loved her. We were going to get married before going to college, as most couples in our city did, so I didn't think twice when she told me she wanted to have sex after our homecoming dance."

"Why did you break up with her if things were so perfect?"

"She broke up with me," I admit. "Two weeks before graduation, I pulled up to her house to drop her off after a date. She told me we had a good run, but she wants to start the next journey of her life single. She wants to meet new people and experience new things, and she can't do that being tied down to me. A country boy from her hometown was not in her future. I was heartbroken," I say, my heart stinging a little. "I felt used, like I was just an object to her. When I got home that night, I saw my acceptance letter to Georgia State. I didn't want to apply, but my counselor insisted they had a great pre-law program, so it didn't hurt to apply. I accepted the offer, and once financial aid confirmed that the most I'd have to come out of pocket per semester was $3,000, I was packed and on my way..."

"I'm sorry that happened to you," Dez says.

"It's whatever. I don't want sympathy. The experience toughened me up. I wasted all that time planning my life with a woman who saw no future with me, so I decided never to do that again. I'll live for me, and what I think is best for my future. I wasn't interested in romance or intimacy, and as I've learned, sex is everywhere."

"So, you decided to act just like her?"

That was a punch to the gut, but somewhat true. "I didn't start off acting like her. I didn't want to date because I thought all girls were the same. But you know how college is. You meet someone you find attractive, y'all go out a few times, and then—"

"Y'all are headed on a weekend getaway in another city before the attraction is gone and you start over again."

We briefly make eye contact then. "I don't consider you dispensable, Dez. You're going to have to believe that." She says nothing, and we spend the next few minutes driving in silence. "If my past bothers you that much, then—"

"Your past doesn't bother me at all. I'm just trying to observe your patterns to predict when things will start heading south for us."

"There's no need to think like that."

"There's no need for you to think about women the way you do. From what I can tell, your parents have a great marriage; you never wanted to replicate that? You never wanted to fall in love with a girl and wake up to her every day? You never wanted someone that felt like home?"

"My parents do have a great marriage, and so do yours. I think love can be a beautiful thing, but it's risky to be that vulnerable with someone. You never know how it'll turn out."

"So, what are we doing?" She whispers.

I know what she means, but I don't want to go there with her right now. Marriage is complicated, and love is messy. I'm with Dez right now because I want to see where we'll end up, but we won't make it far if we don't figure out long term goals for our future.

"We're about to start a weekend getaway. You deserve it for passing all your midterms, and I could really use a break from work. Let's enjoy what we have."

She smiles. "Okay, so I've researched this hotel. It's an adult-only resort, and every room has a privacy balcony. Did you get us a standard or deluxe room?"

I side eye her, insulted by the fact that she hasn't realized that I enjoy the finer aspects of life. "I reserved a two-bedroom penthouse suite." She gives me a look of astonishment, and I chuckle. "I know the owner from a conference in Virginia. He hooked me up with a discount. Have you looked at the amenities? You should plan out our itinerary."

"Yes! There are four pools, four hot tubs, a movie theatre, bowling, mini-golf, and an arcade. So, after we get in and settle down, we can head straight to the beach since we're not far from it. I've been thinking..."

I shake my head and adjust the cruise control in the rental. There are some scars I'm going to have to be comfortable sharing with Dez even if I don't want to. Though it's the opposite of what a divorce lawyer should brag about, all of my clients don't finalize their divorces. Sometimes, all they need is an unbiased third party to help them talk through their rough patches. Sure, I lose more money that way, but I'm satisfied knowing two people who love each other are going to give their marriage another shot than go into the world miserable. Communication is key, and it's been my experience that what's not said does more damage than what is.

Chapter 8: Dezzy

April 5, 2015

"What's on the agenda for today?" Jus asks while joining me on the private balcony.

I had been sunbathing while he was in the shower. Lifting my sun hat and lowering my shades, I glance at him and shrug. He's only wearing basketball shorts and slides.

"Today is a free day. We can stay indoors and relax," I answer.

Nodding, he plops down in the recliner beside me. "There are a ton of things to do in the hotel. There's bowling, an arcade, and a movie theater," he reminds.

"I'll do any one of those things with you. I'm always down for quality time."

Previously, Justin and I have always been able to kick it, but this getaway unlocked a depth of intimacy between us. While here, we swam in the ocean, made sandcastles on the beach, and even did karaoke in the rooftop bar. Justin made sure I enjoyed myself—even allowing me to order room service and taking drinks out of the suite's refrigerator. I told him he didn't have to spoil me like this. He argued that this is how he usually vacations; he just doesn't do this when he's with my family because he doesn't want to seem haughty.

In turn, as is all I know to do, I took care of him. I applied his sunscreen and insect repellent. I made sure he stayed hydrated and didn't pig out during all three meals. I made sure he purchased items for himself when we went shopping and not just for his family, friends, and rude secretary.

"Let's do the arcade, and then a movie," I suggest, breaking his silence. "Your pick."

He slides his chair closer to mine and takes one of my hands in his. "Did you get a lot of cool shots this weekend?"

"Sure did. Wanna see?" I ask, reaching for my camera. I display the pictures before he replies.

"That's a terrible shot of me," he cringes while taking the camera from me to get a closer look of him singing karaoke.

I chuckle. "That's the face you make when you're trying to sing like Bruno Mars," I say, referring to his attempt at "Talking to the Moon."

"Your camera's just old," he complains, scrolling through the other pictures. "I would've looked better if you used the one I bought you."

He stops on a picture of me then. "I didn't know you took this," I say, taking the camera from him for a better look.

Justin shrugs. "I thought you looked nice, so I snapped it."

The picture is of me trying on a powder blue, one-strap formal dress at the mall. The slit stopped just before my upper thigh, and a diamond belt encircled the waist.

"The store's lights caused a glare. If you adjusted the settings like this," I say, showing him what I mean, "then there wouldn't have been a glare. How about I give you lessons?"

"Instead of teaching me how to use this camera, why don't you take pictures with the one I bought? I bet there wouldn't have been a glare without having to adjust the settings."

"I'm still waiting on a special event to use it," I sigh, putting the camera back on the table. "Maybe graduation."

"Graduation is in a couple of weeks. Are you ready?"

"I've been ready since the semester began."

Justin chuckles. "You don't want to get your master's?"

"I wouldn't even go back to school for a certificate," I say before we both laugh.

"So, what's the plan for after graduation?"

After exhaling, I do a lip flutter. Justin looks at me.

"I've been applying to internships and entry-level positions for journals, magazines, and radio stations. I haven't heard back from a single soul. I've even flirted with the idea of applying to photography companies, but they all want experience."

"Then get experience," he commands, looking into my eyes.

"You make it seem like experience is just waiting on the corner outside. One needs to be provided the opportunity to achieve experience in order to obtain experience."

"You don't have to wait until someone gives you a chance to get experience, Dez. You have two cameras, tons of knowledge, and an overstuffed portfolio of pictures of friends, family, and nature stored in a hard drive. You have experience; you need exposure."

"I don't even know where to start," I admit, breaking eye contact.

"It's grad season. Offer graduation packages. Shoot around campus, downtown, or a nearby park. Offer only digital copies and differentiated prices based on one or multiple locations. You could also edit different backgrounds, couldn't you? With digital editing or something?"

Sure, that sounds like a great idea, but... "That's a lot, Justin. That would mean putting myself out there; advertising, socializing, and showing off my skills. It's overwhelming. I don't know if I'm ready for that."

"If you don't take a chance on yourself, then no one else will take a chance on you. You have to invest in yourself before anyone else does."

Dang. He's right. A little too psychological, but right.

"I have the ability to do that," I finally say. "I may have to take some days off from work, but I have the skills to do so."

"Of course you do," he encourages, lying back in the chair. "And you can start an online blog, showcasing your talent and write articles like a journalist."

"And what about you?" I inquire?

"What about me?" He asks, closing his eyes.

"Have you given up on becoming a criminal lawyer?" I ask, running my hand down his chest.

"No."

"Then why haven't you become one yet?"

Shrugging, he stops me from caressing his chest and pulls me onto him. Justin has been very affectionate during this trip. We only shared a bed once during the trip, and that was only because we ordered room service after an intense surfing lesson and fell asleep on his bed after eating. Aside from that, he's been emotionally and physically available to me. Not sexually, though. He's steadfast about us abstaining, especially because we're still on two different pages about marriage. I often wonder if his attentiveness is his way of coping with his urges, or if he's always been like this. Justin has never brought any women around my family since we've met him. We all figured it was out of respect for us because he knew he didn't see a future with them.

"Why haven't you invested in yourself?" I ask again.

"I guess I'm a little scared. What if I'm not as good a criminal attorney as I am as a divorce attorney?"

I've always characterized Justin as overly confident. He isn't cocky, but he'll definitely stare death in the face rather than cower away. He moves as if the direction he's heading in is the only right one. When he teaches me how to play a new game or enlightens me about a random legal term I discovered on social media, he does it so knowledgeably and assuredly that I take it as gospel truth.

"Why wouldn't you be good at it? You're amazing now."

"But that's a whole different ballfield, Dez. People's lives, whether or not they go to jail, it all depends on me." He anxiously rubs my back; this must make him very uneasy.

"It doesn't solely depend on you, babe. It depends on God and our justice system being unbiased."

"But sometimes it is biased. You know how unfair the justice system in this country can be," he passionately reminds.

"I know, but you can't fix America by yourself. All you can do is pray before each case and defend to the best of your ability. You'll always feel unworthy if you do stuff in your own strength. You know you're unstoppable when you tap into the power within."

His back rubs slow to a steady pace as he ponders on my wise words.

"Let me offer a plea bargain." He's been using more jargon to test if I've been retaining anything from his law lessons, but I know plea bargains from all my years of watching *Monk*.

"I'm listening."

"You agree to soft launch your photography company—"

"My what?"

"It's a company, Dez. You're finna offer business services, so you can start off as an LLC. You have a ton of friends and associates. Ask them to help you advertise and offer them discounted prices in return. Word will spread around campus in no time."

He's right. GSU has over 30,000 students, and though I'm not a campus celebrity, I do know a slew of people from the various organizations I'm in, the activities and events I participate in, and from my three semesters with the campus newspaper and radio station.

"What's your part of the deal?" I ask.

"I'll resume transitioning to a criminal attorney."

"What does that look like?"

"Mostly familiarizing myself with current laws and gaining experience."

"Doesn't seem too bad."

He shrugs. "Then there's always the issue of waiting for someone to take a chance on me."

"It'll happen at the right time. Just prepare yourself so that you won't be caught off guard when the time comes."

"Okay," he says, kissing my forehead.

My phone vibrates before I can say anything else. Justin's phone vibrates as I reach for mine. Romeo sent a message to the family group chat.

"Whoa!" I exclaim, sitting up.

Justin smiles. "Good for him."

> **Big Bro: Guess who's getting married?**

Attached to his text is a picture of him and Jane. She's extending her hand to the camera, showing off an engagement ring.

"He looks so happy," I compliment, staring at my brother's smile. It's been months since I've seen it.

> **Mom: Congratulations!**

A message from Romeo pops up as I'm typing his congratulatory response.

> **Big Bro: Buy your tickets now. We're getting married this week.**

"What?!" I yell just as Dad texts the same thing in the chat.

> **Big Bro: Wednesday or Thursday in Brooklyn. Working out the details now.**

Now? Today is Sunday, and Justin and I still have one more day of vacation left. Plus, how high are plane tickets?

Justin's phone buzzes as I'm still processing my brother's incomprehensible message.

"Hey, bro. Congrats," Justin greets, putting the call on speaker.

"Thanks, man. I need a favor."

"What's up?"

"I wanna get married on the Brooklyn Bridge. Where do I start?"

Justin scoffs. "You start thirty days ago, man. That's how long the processing time is."

There Justin goes, speaking as confidently as ever. He's never practiced in New York. How does he know that? I think.

"Damn. I didn't know," Rome replies, disappointedly.

"I have some New York contacts. Let me see if I can pull some strings."

"Why the sudden rush?" I ask.

"It's not a rush." Romeo chuckles. "This is long overdue. The last month and a half without Jane has been hell. I don't ever wanna lose her again."

"Marriage isn't a way to keep her locked up like a pet in a cage," I inform.

"Dang, Dezzy, do you not like Jane or something?" Romeo asks.

He doesn't bother to question why Justin and I are together, but inquires about how I feel about his new *fiancée?*

"I just want to make sure you know what you're doing this time," I confess.

"We both do," Justin adds, holding my hand.

"Marriage isn't my way of keeping Jane under lock and key. I'd wait up to a year if she asked me to. I'm just eager to spend my life with her."

"And I'm just as eager too!" Jane chimes in. "Stressed about finding a dress but excited."

"I gotta make some calls, Rome. I'll let you know something by tonight. I'm not making any promises though, so you better have a backup plan," Justin instructs.

"Thanks, man," Romeo says, before hanging up.

"Damn," Justin says before chuckling. "Romeo's really finna marry her."

My phone vibrates, and I see a private message from Romeo.

Big Bro: Will you sing at our ceremony?

I immediately go to the eye roll emoji, but before I can send it, another message from him arrives.

> Big Bro: Please, lil' sis?

How could I ever tell my loving brother no?

> Me: Fine, but if Jane turns you into a zombie again, I'm finna handle her myself.

Romeo sends three laughing emojis, and I smile.

"I guess you'll get to see me in that dress again," I say, glancing at Justin. Blushing, he licks his lips.

Chapter 9: Dezzy

April 7, 2015

"Welcome to New York, Justin," Mom says as we stand on the sidewalk in front of JFK airport.

"Why is it so loud?" Justin asks, wincing.

Cars honk as they protest the pedestrians in the crossway. Taxi drivers yell out "need a ride" to innocent tourists who have no idea how much the fare from here to down the block will cost. Tons of people stand nearby, talking on the phone. Others wave their hands and yell frantically in order to spot their rides.

"It's New York, baby," I say, walking to the edge of the sidewalk.

Romeo's car stops in front of me a few seconds later. I anxiously smile as the tinted passenger window rolls down. My smile turns into a frown when I see Jane in the driver's seat.

"Hey, y'all!" she warmly greets while popping the trunk.

"Why don't you sit up front and get to know your new sister-in-law better?" Justin teases as he takes my duffle bag.

Sucking my teeth, I get in the back. "Mom can bond with her new daughter-in-law," I mumble.

Mom does in fact sit in the passenger seat, leaving me in the back between Dad and Justin.

"It's so great to see you again," Mom says, hugging Jane as she peels away from the curb.

"It's nice to see you again too, Ms. Rose." "It's nice seeing all of you again," Jane says, glancing at each of us through the rearview mirror.

"Rome must've had to work today," Justin inquires.

"One of his clients asked to reschedule last minute, so he asked me to take airport duty. Don't worry, he'll be off early enough for the festivities you planned."

"What festivities?" I ask, glancing at Justin.

"C'mon, Dez. You know I can't divulge that information with the bride around."

"I'm not worried," Jane says, still smiling. "We have our own festivities to partake in."

"Are you sure your parents have enough room for us?" Mom asks Jane. "We have family in Canarsie we can stay with."

"There's plenty of room, and my mom can't wait to meet you. We're headed to the house now so you and Dezzy can drop your luggage off, and then we'll pop up on Romeo at the gym."

Mom and I would be spending the night with Jane, her mom, and her sister, while Dad and Justin kick it at Romeo's apartment with Jane's dad and brother. This is supposed to be their way of having bachelor and bachelorette parties. I opted to skip, but Justin told me to be nice, so I will... try to at least.

***

After Jane parks by Atlantic Mall, we follow her to Romeo's gym. I want to say it feels good to be back home, but I feel like an alien walking down what were once familiar streets. No one stops for anything here. Pedestrians cross despite the signal telling them not to. Cars drive in the bus lane and honk as soon as the light turns green. Why in the world would my brother move back here?

"Here we are," Jane says, opening a glass, black-framed door.

A bell rings as we enter, and people on the gym floor briefly glance in our direction.

"Hey, Jane," a dark-skinned, muscular man greets. He's a little on the short side, with a tapered cut and twists in his head.

"Hey, Raph. Where's Romeo?"

"He's finishing up with a client. This must be his family."

Jane introduces us to Raph and introduces him to us as Romeo's assistant manager. Rome's gym has hardly been open for a year, yet he's doing well enough to hire an assistant manager.

"I'll see you next week," Romeo says.

We all shift to face him. He's walking a female client out, and his mouth drops open when he sees us.

"I can show myself out," the woman says, walking to the door.

"You just gonna stand there and stare at us with your mouth wide open?" Dad asks.

Rome shakes his head and throws his hands around Dad before hugging Mom.

"What are you guys doing here?" He asks as Mom kisses his cheek.

"Were you not the one who invited us here for your wedding?" I sassily ask.

Chuckling, Romeo pulls me in for a warm hug. I can't help but smile and hug him back as tightly as I can.

"I missed you," I confess.

It catches him off guard because he hesitates as he lets me go. "You just saw me last month, little sis. Don't get all mushy now."

"That wasn't the real you," I whisper as he daps up Justin.

"I ain't even finna lie, your gym is fire," Justin compliments.

The gym floor is fairly packed. There are people on the exercise machines, lifting weights in front of the mirror, doing crunches on mats, and fighting punching bags and training dummies. The gym has a black concrete floor, and the walls are painted orange.

"Does that mean I can get you to work out while you're here?" Romeo teases Justin.

"You'll have to take it slow," Justin nervously chuckles. "I haven't worked out much since you left."

"Ain't that the truth," I say, lightly punching his arm.

Jane glances between me and Justin but says nothing.

"I'm very proud of you, Romeo," Dad says, still in awe.

"It's truly amazing to see your dream become reality," Mom says, and she's right. Rome has been talking about owning a gym since his freshman year at Georgia State.

"Why don't you show them your newly renovated boxing ring?" Jane suggests.

Romeo looks at her, and it's like she's the only thing in his world that exists.

"You're going to challenge me to a match in front of my family?" He asks, walking to her.

"Yeah. I'll let you win this time," she teases as he takes her hands in his.

"Guess this is the last time I'll see you until tomorrow," he tells her. "I can't wait."

Jane blushes as Romeo leans in to kiss her.

"Why don't you give her a chance?" Justin asks, distracting me from the make-out session. "She doesn't seem that bad."

"I guess this is where we split ways," I say.

Justin brushes a kiss on my forehead before walking to Romeo. "Enough of that," he says, pushing Romeo away from Jane. "It's my first time in New York, and I don't plan on watching you kiss your fiancée the whole time."

Laughing, Jane gives Romeo his car keys before joining me and Mom.

"The men will probably be here a little while longer. Do y'all wanna take the subway or a cab to my parents' house?" She asks.

***

"It should be nice and quiet in here for you," Jane says, showing me to the room furthest from the street. "You shouldn't hear sirens or any other sounds from the city that never sleeps."

An oval archway gives access to a quaint bedroom. There's hardwood flooring, just like in the other rooms on the first floor of Jane's parents' brownstone. A beautifully made queen-sized bed with a headboard is pushed against the wall. There's a window with a view of the backyard in the corner, and a huge, wooden dresser is across from the bed with a TV on it.

"Thanks," I say, dropping my duffle bag on the dresser.

"I'm right upstairs if you need anything. I didn't expect our night to end so early, but it seems like our mothers are having more fun than we are."

"I'm not surprised they hit it off," I admit. "They're around the same age and grew up in Brooklyn around the same time. Had they gone to the same school, they probably would've been best friends."

"Then Romeo and I could've met much sooner," Jane says, walking to the door.

"Do you actually love my brother?"

Jane stops and faces me. "Of course, I do."

"He's already been through a lot, so if you're planning to bail on him when times get tough—"

"What's your real issue with me, Dezzy?" Jane asks, cutting me off and walking toward me.

I've heard the countless stories about how good of a fighter she is, but I refuse to be intimidated.

"I wasn't able to protect my brother the first go-around, but I don't plan on letting him make the same mistake twice."

"And you think him marrying me is a mistake?"

"I think him marrying the wrong person is a mistake. I don't know you well enough to say if that's you, and this stunt y'all are pulling doesn't give me much time to figure it out."

"Maybe you should try to get to know me instead of putting up a brick wall."

I roll my eyes, and she scoffs.

"I can tell you're protective of those closest to you. The way you and Justin interacted let me know you don't play about him either."

My eyes widen; could she tell that Justin, and I are a couple? I promised him I would keep my mouth shut because he promised me he would tell Romeo during this trip. I definitely don't want to tell Jane about us because I can't risk her blabbing her mouth.

"Romeo thinks very highly of you, Desdemona. He mentions your accomplishments quite often, and he can't wait to attend your graduation. I know he'd like it if we got along, but I won't beg for a relationship if you're not interested in one."

We stare at each other for a while. Jane is a few inches taller than me, light-skinned, with curly hair. For as strong-willed as she is, her face is soft and welcoming. It's not surprising to see why my brother fell for her. I don't have a shortage of friends, but from the little I know about her, she's already a better person than Donna. Donna didn't care to give me the time of day. She was cordial with me in front of family but treated me like an annoyance when we were alone. Jane doesn't seem to change from person to person. I know that much from the way she chatted with my parents during her visit in January.

"Did you find a nice dress?" I whisper, breaking eye contact.

She smiles. "Yes, and thankfully, the parents of my childhood friend altered it in a matter of hours for me."

"How are you going to wear your hair?" I ask, sitting on the bed, giving a small smile to lighten the mood.

Jane sits beside me and goes into detail about a style with a side part and barrel curls. I then ask her about makeup.

"I'll just use Vaseline and lipstick."

I want to slap her. "Vaseline and lipstick? This is your wedding day!"

Jane chuckles. "You sound like my mom. I could do a little foundation and mascara."

"I can do your makeup," I offer. Jane raises an eyebrow. "I won't have you looking like a clown," I assure. "After Justin jumped through all these hoops to grant y'all special permission to get married on the Brooklyn Bridge, it'll be a shame if the wedding doesn't happen."

Jane smiles. "Fine. Thanks." Then her face expresses that a lightbulb went off. Her lips part to ask a question, but she stops, deciding not to push it.

"Have you and Rome always been on the same page about marriage?"

Jane gives me a skeptical look. "Honestly, I didn't know Romeo would want to get married so soon after leaving his ex-wife. I thought we would at least date for a year before marriage was on the table. I definitely didn't expect him to propose the night we rekindled our relationship, especially after a month's breakup."

"So, you wanted to wait longer before getting married?"

She shrugs. "I would continue living my life until my season of marriage arrived. Did I expect my season to arrive in seven months? No. Am I going to welcome it with open arms? Absolutely. Why is marriage on your mind?"

I shrug then. "I've always wanted to get married, but what do you do when the person you want to marry thinks marriage is foolish?"

"I find a new person," Jane answers. I look at her, shocked. "No one can change my ideals about something, so I operate under the guise that I can't change anyone else's. You don't want to force someone into marriage, nor should you forfeit your desire to be married. In the end, both parties will be miserable."

"Hmph," I pout. I don't like having this heart-to-heart with Jane but having an unbiased outsider's opinion is valuable.

"So, do you want to keep having sappy conversations, or do you wanna put your shoes back on and have a night on the town? It is my last night as a single woman, after all."

"Well, I've never explored New York as an adult."

Chapter 10: Justin

April 8, 2015

Aside from the music on the radio, the drive to the Brooklyn Bridge is quiet. Thankfully, I was able to get Romeo and Jane forty-five minutes on the bridge because I had contacts with people in high places. I'm glad to make his dream come true, but I feel guilty. Romeo and I have shared everything with each other since becoming friends. Even the messy things bros don't talk about, like the truth about his marriage to Donna and how I feel about Alana. Not being able to tell him about me and Dez sucks.

Keeping him in the dark about a significant part of my life feels like betrayal, even more so because it's his sister that I'm dating. I'd love to get his insight on the marriage quandary Dez, and I are in. Should I just break up with her and let her find the man who isn't scared of marriage? Commitment I have no problem with, but marriage? That's agreeing to the possibility of failure. At least with dating no vows are involved, but with marriage. I shake my head. There's too much to lose, and I'm not even talking about alimony.

The car comes to a stop, and I look around. I see a suspension bridge in the distance and realize we've arrived.

"How are you feeling, man?" I ask Romeo as we get out of the car.

"I feel good, bro," he smiles.

"You look good too," his dad compliments while grabbing the Bluetooth speaker and microphone Romeo borrowed from his gym.

"Thanks for coming. I wouldn't want to get married without y'all," Rome says as we start walking.

"I wouldn't miss this for the world," I say, throwing my arm around him. "I told you I got your back."

Romeo's steps slow until he comes to a halt.

"You okay?" I ask.

"What did you want to tell me?" He asks, moving from under my arm.

"What are you talking about?"

"The day after Valentine's Day, when I was in Georgia, you kept trying to tell me something, but I wouldn't give you the chance. What was it?"

My smile leaves my face.

"I want to tell you about this girl I've been dating since Valentine's Day," I admit. I wanted to bring it up last night during his party, but everyone was having such a great time that I didn't want to sour the mood. I also didn't want to risk Romeo going bat crazy and giving Jane's father a reason to call off the wedding.

"You let a girl hook you for two months? You usually love them and leave them." He chuckles, but I don't.

"She's different."

Romeo stares at me, his playful demeanor gone. "You should've brought her with you."

"Actually, I—"

"Actually, why don't we head up to the bridge to ensure everything is ready for Jane's arrival?" Pop suggests cutting me off.

I briefly look at Pop before returning to Romeo. "Your dad's right. I can tell you about her later."

Nodding, Romeo takes his phone out and walks a few steps ahead.

"You really think a few minutes before his wedding is the best time to tell him you're dating his sister?" Pop whispers to me.

"This is the first opportunity I've had to do it."

"Find another one," Pop says before lightly hitting my back. It hurts a little, but only because I'm sore from the workout routine Rome put me through at the gym yesterday.

We resume the walk to the bridge silently where Romeo greets the pastor and photographer. The photographer snaps some pictures of Romeo and the pastor before taking some with me and my best friend. I'm genuinely happy for him, and I have a feeling that this marriage is going to last. My phone buzzes, and I open a text from Dez.

"The girls are here," I tell Romeo.

A nervous look comes across his face, and I laugh. It's funny seeing a man as confident as him get nervous over seeing his bride. A car door opens and slams as I turn on the speaker and connect the microphone via Bluetooth. A figure in a dress cloaked by the sunlight approaches us. Romeo walks beside me, obviously hoping it's Jane. His face flattens when he sees it's Dez. My mouth drops when I see how beautiful she looks in the powder blue dress she bought in Savannah. Her hair is curled and parted to the side, and she's wearing a full face of makeup with nude lip gloss.

"You don't have to look so happy to see me," she says, rolling her eyes at Romeo's disappointment.

I pick my mouth off the floor, stand up, and clear my throat. Dez gazes at me as she and Romeo hug. She bites her lip as she takes me in. Clearly, she loves the way I look in my black tuxedo. Romeo told us there isn't a dress code since the wedding is last minute; he and Jane are saving all those formalities for their official wedding in August. I can't peel my eyes away from Dez, even as the photographer takes pictures of her and Romeo.

Dez walks to my side once she's free.

"Got everything working?" She asks.

I hand her the mic. "You're so beautiful."

She blushes so hard that her cheeks almost turn red. Or maybe it's her makeup playing tricks on me.

"Stop that, Justin. Unless you've told Romeo already," she fishes, raising an eyebrow.

I shake my head, and she pouts. Even that's adorable.

"I'm glad you like the dress though," she says, spinning around. "We had a little malfunction, so Jane's mom had to—"

"Whoa," I say, spinning her back around. "What's this?" I ask, looking at the back of her upper left shoulder.

She chuckles. "You mean the tattoo? Jane and I got them last night."

I raise an eyebrow. "Jane got a Georgia peach tattoo?"

"Don't be silly," Dez says, facing me. "I got a Georgia one, and she got a New York apple one. She called me a traitor for getting a Georgia one, but—" Dez stops talking when she notices the way I'm looking at her. "What's wrong? You don't approve?"

"Nah, I'm thinking about the fact that I now have to kiss you here," I say, gently touching her new tattoo, "and here," I say, touching the older one.

"Justin!" She whisper-yells. "Leave me alone before you make me forget the words to the song."

I open my mouth to object, but Jane's mom and siblings arrive then, and the pastor orders everyone to their positions.

"Go stand next to Rome, with your fine self," Dez says, winking at me.

I shake my head while making my way to Romeo. Bump what Pop said; I may just tell Romeo right now that Dez and I are dating. A few seconds later, Dez starts singing "At Last" by Etta James, and I get chills. Dez has always been the family singer, but today, she sings as if she personally empathizes with the lyrics. Romeo's and everyone else's eyes are on Jane, but I can't take my eyes off Dez. She's really into the song too because her body is swaying, and her free hand is gesticulating as she sings.

When she finishes, she walks over to us and stands by her mother, and the pastor starts the ceremony. I wink at Dez, and she blushes as she puts some hair behind her ears. I mouth "you did great" to her, and she mouths "thank you." Smiling, I mouth, "What are you doing after this?"

The pastor clears his throat, and I look at him, like a deer caught in headlights. Romeo and Jane are giving him the same look, and I relax, realizing they must've been doing the same thing Dez and I were. Chuckling, I take one last look at Dez before giving Romeo my full attention.

***

"Do you want to go back to the Salgado house to grab some lunch?" I ask Dez, referring to Jane's mom's lunch invitation.

She shrugs. "Think I'd rather explore New York. It's been a while since I've been home."

"Why don't you show me around then?" I ask, wrapping my arms around her waist.

She brings a hand to my cheek just as we hear a camera flash. We both look in the direction it came from as the photographer takes another one of us.

"That's a beautiful shot," she tells us. "Think I'll keep it." The last time I saw the photographer, she was trailing behind Romeo and Jane as they went to Rome's car.

"Or you can delete it," I say, letting Dez go.

"Wait," Jack, Jane's younger brother, snickers, "are you two dating?"

"Yes," Dez and I answer. At this point, I won't deny it to anyone.

"What did Romeo say?" Jane's mother asks.

"Nothing yet, so could you please delete that picture?" I ask the photographer.

"I think it should make it into the album," Ms. Rose taunts. "A picture is worth a thousand words."

"It's fine, Jus," Dez says, taking my hand in hers. "That can be our first wedding gift to them."

Relaxing, I exhale and nod.

"Are you two joining us for lunch?" Ms. Rose asks.

I look at Dez before answering, "Nah. We're going on an adventure of our own."

She smiles at me before looking at her mother. "Can I have my flats and camera, Ma?" She asks, stretching her hand out. Ms. Rose produces a pair of flats for Dez, and she leans on me as she takes off her heels and gives them to her mother.

"You still know your way around New York?" I ask as she steps into her flats.

She shrugs and slings her old camera across her body. "What I don't know, the GPS does."

***

"Are you going to finish your cheesecake?" I ask Dez after our waitress at Junior's gives me the bill.

"I don't think I have any more room," she whines. "I get bloated and full so quickly. I hate it."

"Just means you get to take home leftovers," I say, leaving two fifties in the checkbook.

"And I'm so tired. I can't believe you had me all over New York."

"Me?" I scoff. "You're the one who wanted to ride the ferry to see Lady Liberty."

"Yes, but you insisted we go see the Empire State Building."

"We're in Manhattan, so why not? I might as well enjoy myself while I'm here." I take a spoonful of her birthday cake cheesecake in my mouth.

"Did you enjoy yourself?" She inquires.

"Excluding all the shopping you did?" I tease.

"I didn't shop that much."

"You shopped so much that we had to stop at the Macy's on 34th Street to buy you a suitcase because your new items won't fit in the duffle bag you brought," I remind her, finishing her dessert.

"Hey, we got stuff for your condo too, since you surprisingly gave me the green light to decorate it," she says as we stand up.

The last few times Dez visited my place, she complained about it looking like an unwelcoming bachelor pad. While shopping today, she began pointing out décor that she thought would look great in the condo. I gave her permission to get a few items, and she got so carried away that she also ordered items to be delivered once we get back.

"But you needed those decorations and to experience that Macy's," Dez continues. "It's iconic; it has a wooden escalator!"

Laughing, I roll my eyes and grab her suitcase as we exit. "Because I haven't been on a wooden escalator before. Anyway, I mostly enjoyed spending time with you."

Her eyes light up. "Really?"

A gentleman walking opposite of us jostles me without saying anything. I turn around to see what his problem is, but he's too busy hurrying off to his destination. I don't know why people live here. I thought I got used to people shoving me on the subway, but on the streets too. Are people in New York too good to learn manners?

I lock hands with Dez as we continue walking down the street. "It was cute having you tell me all sorts of interesting facts about New York and sharing with me the memories you have here. I enjoyed you giving me more lessons on how to use your camera as we viewed sites. I even liked the little rundown escalator you took me on."

She pushes me playfully. "So, what are you saying? I know how to show you a good time."

"No. I'm saying, I love being around you. Whether we're lounging around like we did the last two days in Savannah, or we're learning how to surf, or singing karaoke, I always have a ball. I like having you in my presence."

She stops walking and looks into my eyes. "I've always enjoyed being around you, Justin, but since we've been dating, being with you feels like a dream come true. You don't get upset when I pick up last-minute shifts at work or decide to sleep over at my friend's houses for days at a time. You don't blow up my phone, but you're always there when I need you. One thing that worried me about our relationship was whether I'll be able to add anything to your life the way you add to mine."

I chuckle. "You're my oasis from reality. I can be who I truly am around you without fear of judgment. You keep me company, you keep me grounded, and you look after me after I've exhausted myself looking after everyone else."

"And I make sure you're not always eating takeout and fast food," she grins.

Damn, Rome was right: how could I let a woman tie me down like this? Have me sharing childhood stories and lifelong fears and aspirations. Not only can Dez pop up at my condo whenever she likes as long as I'm home, but now she has permission to decorate as she sees fit? Love is bittersweet, and people just willingly choose to feel like this? They're crazy... and I just added myself to the number.

"I'm so glad I have you in my life," I confess.

"You've always had me in your life, Justin," she says, wrapping her arms around me.

"I'm glad I have you as my girlfriend. You reminded me of the pleasures of being committed to one person and..." I look away and exhale.

"And what?" She asks, gently turning my face back to hers.

"And the excitement of planning a future with someone." She gasps, and I look into her eyes. "I love you, Desdemona."

She stares at me, not moving or breathing. I chuckle.

"I just admitted that I've fallen for you, and you're gonna give me the silent treatment?"

She unnecessarily stands on her tippy toes and brings her lips centimeters away from mine. "I love you too, Justin." Then she kisses me. Right in Times Square, amid strangers sucking their teeth because we're in their way, she kisses me, and it's the best one I've ever had.

Her eyes are watery when we part. I begin to ask why she's crying, but she talks first.

"We better get back to Brooklyn. Jane's family was nice enough to host us, so we shouldn't return to their house too late."

Looking around at the monitors in Times Square, I see that it's minutes to nine.

"Did you pack all your belongings in your duffle bag before you left this morning, or did you leave a mess?"

"I never leave a mess," she says, hitting my chest. I give her a skeptical look, and she rolls her eyes. "I packed my stuff because I'm a guest at the Salgado residence."

"Text your parents and ask them to bring your bag to the airport tomorrow. Tell them we'll meet them there."

"What? Why?"

"Because we're going to a hotel," I say, turning toward the street and hailing a cab.

We aren't scheduled to be at the airport until noon tomorrow for our four o'clock flight. Dez does as I instructed while I talk to the taxi driver about taking us to the nearest five-star hotel.

Chapter 11: Justin

April 23, 2015

I loosen my tie as I walk through the courtroom's French oak doors. This case lasted longer than I anticipated. My client, Jasper Howel, just divorced his wife for infidelity. She'd been a stay-at-home wife for twelve years and wanted spousal as well as child support. Jasper and his ex-wife were using the same lawyer, but he sought me out when he suspected foul play. He was right. The other lawyer wanted the ex-wife to have everything, even if it wasn't due to her. I'm glad the judge saw through the cow manure. Not only is Jasper walking away with primary custody of their three children, but he isn't required to pay spousal support either.

I shake my head. I'd flip my wig if I provided my woman with the opportunity to be a stay-at-home wife and she cheated on me and destroyed our family. As I'm heading to the exit, I spot a tearful mother helping who looks like her son adjust his tie. She's short, with her hair pulled in a bun and wearing a Sunday dress. The dress is worn, though it's spruced up with a belt and pearls. Her son towers over her. He's fair-skinned, and though his hair is freshly cut, his curly hair still prevails. He's wearing a suit that's a size too big for him.

"Let me get that," I say, approaching them. "I'm Justin Campbell. What's with all the gloomy faces?"

The mother hesitantly steps away as she and her son make eye contact. I lift the son's collar and begin adjusting the tie.

"He has a trial today. We're..." The mother stops talking as her lip trembles.

The son looks at her, worry in his eyes. "It'll be fine," he lies. My five years of practicing have taught me how to quickly pickup on lies.

"I'm an attorney, so please feel free to tell me what you feel comfortable with. I would like to help."

"I'm on trial for a crime I didn't commit. I fit a description, so now I'm here. We were supposed to meet my lawyer, but we haven't seen him since arriving. Mom thinks the lawyer is going to throw the case."

I give him a skeptical look. It's not like I haven't heard about shady lawyers, but "Why would he throw the case?"

"He was assigned to us because we can't afford a lawyer of our own," the mom explains.

"We've only spoken to him twice before today," the son says. "He seems to be against me too."

"What are your names?" I inquire, dropping the neatly fixed tie.

"Diego Sanford, and this is my mother, Mrs. Sanford."

"Why don't y'all just hang tight for a moment?" I suggest, gesturing to a bench.

They look at each other before having a seat. I speed-walk to Brenda's office. She's a high-ranking clerk who's been sweet on me since I started practicing. She's an older, attractive lady; my type... my former type. I definitely would've taken her on a date, had we not worked so closely together. After passing the bar, I vowed to never mix work and romance. As much as I would've enjoyed spending a few evenings with Brenda, I knew no good would ever come out of it. She's probably ready to settle down, and I just like having a good time... at least I did before Dez.

"Hey, beautiful," I say, knocking on her open office door.

She smiles from ear to ear. "Good morning, Mr. Campbell. How can I help you?"

"What can you tell me about the Sanford case?" I ask, approaching her desk.

She types away on her computer before turning the screen toward me.

"Diego Sanford. He was picked up and booked two months ago for assaulting a woman one night. He claims he didn't do it, but she picked him out from a police lineup. It's Donnovan's case; why are you asking about it?"

"I think I'll take it off his hands."

Brenda scoffs as she turns the screen toward her. "Mrs. Sanford is a widow, not a divorcee. She needs a criminal attorney, not a divorce lawyer."

Brenda never holds anything back, a redeeming quality of hers. "They told me they've only spoken to Donnovan once. This is community service to him; we both know he doesn't really want this case."

She clicks her mouse before sitting back in her chair with her arms folded. "Haven't seen you in a while, Justin. Divorce rates are still high, so I know work hasn't been slow."

I chuckle as her printer starts up. "I've been on vacation. Went to Savannah for a while and then to New York."

She raises an eyebrow. "Two lucky women in one week? Must be nice."

I blush. "One woman," I correct.

She raises both eyebrows then as her printer beeps. "Clear it with Donnovan, and I'll have all the information you need tucked away in a folder when you get back."

Nodding, I get up and head to the lounge—the most likely place Donnovan will be since he has to defend soon. I don't necessarily have to clear anything with him. I only have to tell him he's no longer on the case.

"Campbell!" Donnovan greets as he and some other lawyers look at me. "What're you doin' here? You usually win your cases and leave."

I step into the lounge and close the door behind me. A cafeteria-style table sits in the middle of the floor. There are two microwaves and refrigerators in the corner. The lounge is dark, partly due to the fact that the blinds are closed, mostly due to its position in the courthouse. I avoid coming in here because a lot of my colleagues only come here to gossip or hook up.

"Let me take the Sanford case off your hands."

Donnovan looks at me, questioningly. "That's an open and shut case. Not to mention, no one's getting a divorce. Why would you want it?"

Because I can do a better job than you can. You pathetic piece of... "I'm testing my hand with criminal cases. If this one is so easy, then it'll make perfect practice for me."

Donnovan shakes his head. "I'm tellin' you, kid, it's meat and potatoes. He was picked out of the lineup. Dante might as well kiss his mother goodbye for the next year."

"Diego," I correct.

"Who?" Donnovan asks, confused.

I shake my head. "His mother asked that I represent them. I'm just giving you a heads up," I say, turning my back to leave.

"Have fun," he cackles as I close the door behind me.

I've never liked Donnovan, mostly because he preys on my vulnerable female clients. The mandatory thirty-day wait period for the divorce to become finalized isn't even up by the time he slips them his number. The worst part? He's married with kids. Marriage is a joke.

Sighing, I head back to Brenda's office. My phone vibrates before I walk in.

> Dez: Finna be late for dinner. How about takeout tonight? I know you miss it.

She's been busy with photoshoots since we returned from New York. We see each other less because she stays on campus more since that's where her customers are, but I'm thrilled that she's doing what she loves.

> Me: Miss you or eating whatever I want? I'll probably be late too. Let's just meet somewhere.

After hitting send, I call Cordelia.

"Stuck in traffic?" she answers.

"I'm probably not going to make it back to the office today. Can you reschedule my 3:40?"

"Sure. Everything okay?"

"I picked up another case."

"What?"

"I'll tell you about it later. Can you apologize to the client for the late notice and offer the next session free?"

"Sure thing," she says before I hang up.

I walk into Brenda's office, and she hands me a folder without saying anything. She's too focused on whatever's on her screen to pay me much attention.

"Thanks. I'll bring you a cup of iced coffee next time I'm here," I promise before walking out.

I lean against the wall outside her office as I read the file in more detail. Diego works for a pizza company. He had just come back to the shop when the night manager sent him on another delivery. According to Diego, he delivered the pizza and came straight back to work. On the other hand, a non-Black woman was assaulted and robbed while Diego was making his delivery. She gave the police a description that barely fits Diego.

Diego's manager and coworkers all vouch that he completed his route and returned to the store, where he stayed until the end of his shift. Based on the delivery address and the location where the woman was attacked, there's no way Diego would've been able to do both at the same time. Either he delivered the pizza, or he assaulted the woman. The customer claims that the pizza was delivered, but she didn't pay attention to the driver. This makes the prosecution think that Diego got someone else to deliver the pizza while he attacked the victim. Diego is a senior in high school, set to attend college on a track scholarship. His family migrated here from the Virgin Islands six years ago. He hasn't been in any trouble since coming here.

Closing the file, I make my way back to the Sanford's. "I'd like to defend you today," I tell them. They look at me in disbelief. "I've read the details, and I strongly believe you have a fighting chance."

Though I've never practiced criminal law, I have conducted relevant research on cases and laws. I can finesse my way through everything else.

"What do you say, Ma?" Diego asks.

Mrs. Sanford stares at me before nodding her head. I smile. I believe in giving everyone a fair, fighting chance, and I despise lawyers who don't have their client's best interest at heart. I glance at my watch; there's less than thirty minutes left until Diego's case.

"Do you have any witnesses?"

"No," Diego replies.

I repress a disappointed sigh. A character witness would've been great, but I'll make things shake without one. An idea pops into my head, and I shoot Cordelia a text message. Afterward, I tell Diego to go into as much detail as possible about the night of the incident. I want to know the shift time, who was there with him, what kind of car he drives, how the delivery went, how the arrest went, and what happened at the police station. No detail is insignificant. I take notes in shorthand, ensuring that I understand everything.

"I think that about does it. Let's head in," I say, standing up.

"Wait," Mrs. Sanford says, taking hold of my hand. "Let's pray."

Diego joins our circle, and his mother begins praying. I've never prayed with a client before, but I definitely pray more in court than I do anywhere else.

"Amen," I say at the end.

Exhaling deeply, I enter the courtroom. Immediately, the judge looks surprised to see me. He's Judge Ken Ruby, an older white man with no plans of retiring anytime soon. He does his fair share of socializing. I ran into him at the politician's party Dez and I attended last month. But from what I hear, as friendly as he is, he plays no favorites when it comes to work.

"Mr. Campbell, it is my understanding that you're now representing Mr. Sanford," Judge Ruby says.

"Correct," I say, showing Mrs. Sanford where to sit before bringing Diego to where we need to sit.

"Very well," Judge Ruby says before starting the case.

The plaintiff's lawyer, Sondra, gives me a baffled look. We've known each other since law school but have never faced off against each other. Judge Ruby summarizes why we're before him today before Sondra gives her opening statement. She cuts straight to the chase, highlighting that her client, Fatima, was walking around her neighborhood a little after seven when a man approached her and demanded that she give him her purse and other valuables.

Fatima attempted to run, but the man cornered her, shoved her to the ground, and took off with her purse. Fatima ran home and told her parents what happened. They called the cops, and she filed a police report. Fatima and Diego live two neighborhoods apart, so when the cops saw Diego leaving for school, they realized he fit the description, so they brought him in, which leads us to where we are today.

I pay careful attention to the words Sondra chooses to use. I also take frequent glances at Fatima, who seems to be nervous about something.

"Mr. Campbell?" Judge Ruby says when it's my turn.

"Picture this: a young man is going about his workday, completing his daily tasks. Suddenly, toward the end of his shift, he's arrested without reason, booked, and denied basic constitutional rights until the next day. He's thrown into a lineup, and it's not until he's identified in the lineup that he's finally privy to the fact that he's been arrested on assault charges simply because neighborhood surveillance, on the other side of town from where the attack occurred, took footage of him in a black hoodie and a black hat. There's nothing linking him to this crime except for the laziness of certain officials in finding the true culprit. Your honor, what we have today is another case of racial profiling. Today, I intend to prove that not only is Mr. Sanford innocent, but also that he's been unjustly accused of this crime."

Judge Ruby sits up then, surprised by my claims. Sondra represses a scoff; years later, and she still can't keep a poker face.

"You've made some strong claims, Mr. Campbell. Especially for someone who just took this case. Ms. Davis, please present your evidence."

Sondra goes to the court TV and plays a video of Fatima's attack. Sondra explains that the footage is from a resident's house, which explains the awkward angle of the video. It's slanted, not giving accurate figure dimensions. Then she plays another video, one of Diego dressed in the same attire as the attacker. I quickly look through the file Brenda gave me. This video is from a grocery store camera, which explains why it's clearer and captures Diego better.

"Cross examination," Judge Ruby calls.

"I'll make this quick," I say, walking from behind the table. "I've always been animated and enthusiastic when defending. "The first video is taken from the neighborhood the defendant was walking in. It's even time-stamped. The second video, however, is missing the time Diego was captured, but more importantly, the only thing it proves is that Diego and the assailant dressed similarly for the weather." Sondra scoffs, and I glance at her. "It's common sense that February is a winter month; are we going to arrest everyone who wears a black hoodie and hat to stay warm?"

"Your honor, the attire played a big role in Mr. Sanders capture; it shouldn't be disregarded as a simple fashion choice."

"But the fact that the grocery store that recorded Diego is a twenty-five-minute drive from where your client was attacked should be disregarded?" I ask Sondra.

She rolls her eyes. "Judge, the second footage was only presented to show that the defendant and assailant were dressed the same."

"Isn't that what I said?" I ask, walking back to my table. "The whole purpose of both videos was to show that the defendant and assailant, whom the prosecution agrees are two different people, were both dressed for winter."

Sondra rolls her eyes and folds her arms. "Your honor, I'd like for my client to take the stand."

Judge Ruby approves us moving forward with the case. Sondra asks Fatima to describe the incident—what happened, how she felt—any and everything to make an emotional appeal. I'm not buying it, though.

Questions race through my mind as I approach Fatima. Before I ask the first one, though, I see Cordelia walk in.

"Your honor, I'd like to request a recess." The judge looks at me as if I had just told him that white men can indeed jump.

"This is a simple bench trial, your honor. I see no reason for a recess," Sondra says.

"Why do you want a recess before the cross-examination?" Judge Ruby asks me.

"My cross-examination is a bit interactive. I'd like time to prepare."

"Interactive?" Sondra scoffs. "This is court, not a classroom."

Ignoring her, I face the judge. "Sir, I'd like to invite a sketch artist in. I'd also like to enter into evidence the sketch art drawn the night of the incident."

"Your honor, the defense is grasping at straws. There's no relevance of having sketches entered now; this isn't arts and crafts."

"I'm giving my client a fair chance. If Ms. Davis is so confident that everything will turn out fine for her and her client, then I don't see what the problem is. I only just got this case an hour ago, and I'm a visual learner. I plan to have the whole story before me and the court today, and in order to do that, I need a brief recess."

The judge thinks for a moment before nodding. "We will take a fifteen-minute recess." He slams the gavel and then gets up to leave.

Sondra walks over to me with her arms folded.

"What are you doing here, Justin?" She stresses every syllable in her annoying cat-like timbre.

"At court? Working. Isn't that what you're doing?"

"Why are you on a bench trial? Did I miss the part about a wealthy divorcee?"

"If I were you, I'd be more concerned with preparing my client for the cross-examination than worrying about whether or not you and Jeff will make it to my office."

Fire engulfs her pupils then. "Jeff and I are fine," she says through gritted teeth.

"Then where's your ring, *Ms. Davis*?"

Sondra glares at me before going back to Fatima. For the life of me I couldn't tell why she hates me. We barely interacted during law school. Our cohort went to a party once; she asked me if I was interested in anybody at school. I laughed and told her no, and the next day she was with Jeff.

"What's her deal?" Cordelia asks, approaching me.

I shrug. "Maybe she's upset about going through a divorce. Did you bring it?"

"Of course I did," she says, handing me a bag.

I instruct Diego and his mother to follow me and Cordelia to a private room, so I can tell them about the rest of my plan.

***

"I want to start by saying I'm terribly sorry this incident happened to you." Standing up, I undo my top blazer button and look at Fatima. Diego is sitting outside the courtroom with an officer, waiting for me to give the cue for them to enter. "That being said, there are some facts I'd like to review. How long have you lived in the neighborhood?"

"Objection," Sondra calls. "Relevance?"

"Overruled, Ms. Davis. Let the defense start the examination," Judge Ruby states.

"I've lived in the neighborhood for about four years."

"Was the night of the incident the first time you walked down that street?" I ask.

"No. I'd frequently walk there. Sometimes at day and sometimes at night."

"Did you always walk alone?"

"Most of the time."

"So, you felt safe in this neighborhood then?"

Fatima looks at Sondra before answering, "Yes."

"Will you tell me about the scenery of the neighborhood?" I ask, leaning on the defense stand.

"What do you mean?" Fatima questions.

"How does it look? What sights do you encounter on your walk? What was so interesting that you had to go down that street?"

"Objection. Compound question."

"She asked for clarification, and I explained what I meant. My original question remains the same: will you tell me about the scenery of the neighborhood?"

"There are houses. There's a playground a street over, but there isn't anything special. It's a typical neighborhood."

"Thank you. How much light was outside on the night of the incident?"

Fatima hesitates while looking at Sondra. "Light?"

I try to be patient. "Allow me to rephrase. The incident happened after eight, and the sun sets around six-thirty in February; how well could you see during your walk?"

"There are streetlights in the neighborhood."

"A lot?" I inquire. If I were the original lawyer, I would've inspected every inch of the neighborhood before today's trial. I also would've re-searched the crime rates there, particularly if there had been any other robberies.

"They're scattered throughout the neighborhood, but not all of them work."

"So, how well was your sight?"

Fatima shrugs. "I walk there every day. I know where everything is. The limited light doesn't bother me."

"Limited light? Now we're getting somewhere. Tell me about your interaction with the assailant."

"I was on my phone, listening to music, when a man walked up to me. He yelled at me to give him my phone and purse. I ran away, but he followed me. He threw me to the ground, grabbed my items, and then left."

"He only spoke to you once?" I ask.

"Yes."

"Only that one line?"

"Yes."

"Describe his voice."

"I can't."

"It was the scariest night of your life, was it not? Tell me how he sounded."

"I don't know," Fatima said, her voice rising. "Deep or raspy. I don't know how to describe a man's voice."

"Your honor, I fail to see what Mr. Campbell is doing other than torturing my client," Sondra says.

"Hurry it along, Mr. Campbell," Judge Ruby demands.

"In the corner are two court-approved sketch artists. I want you to describe, to the best of your ability and in as much detail as possible, the assailant."

"Objection!" Sondra exclaims. "We already have a sketch on file from the first time she did this."

"Indulge me, please, your honor. I am going somewhere with this."

"Overruled. Young lady, describe your attacker."

Fatima closes her eyes and takes a deep breath. "He was wearing a black skully, a black hoodie, and dark blue jeans. His eyes were...small, brown, and round. His jaw was rigid and tight. He was about my height, but his muscles made him look stronger. His voice was so mean and brutal. He yelled at me to give him my belongings. I didn't see a weapon on him, so I ran away—up the street to where I knew there were streetlights and people. He threw me on the ground and ripped my phone from my hand. His thick eyebrows made him look even more terrifying, so after he took my phone, I threw my purse at him and covered my face and head, hoping he'd leave me alone. When I looked up, he was gone." Fatima opens her eyes, and tears fall.

I grab a box of tissue and hand it to her. "Thanks for sharing. Obviously, it's still a traumatic incident for you," I say before walking over to the TV. "Your honor, here is the original sketch. It's similar to what the plaintiff described, but there are some features not presented, like the thick eyebrows mentioned. I would like to present the sketches done in court as the plaintiff was recounting her attack. May I approach the bench?"

"You may. Ms. Davis, you may also."

I take the sketches from the two artists and place them in front of the judge and Sondra.

"Sir, not only are the sketches different from one another despite both artists hearing the same account, but they are also different from the sketch on the screen."

"What's your point?" Sondra mumbles.

I decide to answer, in spite of her unprofessionalism. "The point is, there is no definite, concrete picture of the attacker. Three different artists drew three different pictures, and may I add that not a single one even remotely resembles my client. There was never a clear enough picture that should've resulted in the arrest of Diego."

"He was chosen in a lineup."

"Your honor, may I ask for one more favor?" I ask, walking away from the bench.

"No more recess; it's late enough in the day as is," Judge Ruby says.

"I would like to dim the lights in the courtroom."

"I've indulged you a little, Mr. Campbell, but you're pushing it."

"Just a little, your honor. After this demonstration, I'll rest my case."

"Do it with the lights on."

Sighing, I nod at Cordelia. She goes outside for a few seconds before returning and taking her seat. A short while later, Diego enters with a court officer by his side. Diego is dressed in the same attire the assailant wore, which is what I asked Cordelia to buy and bring to the courtroom for me.

"Is this how your attacker looked?" I ask, walking to Fatima.

She stares at Diego for a long time. "The clothes are the same."

"Yes, the clothes are the same, but is this the physique of the man who attacked you that night? Are his eyes the same, his eyebrows, his..." I look at Diego then and nod my head.

"Give me your phone and purse!" Diego says in his most menacing voice.

Fatima jumps, and the audience gasps.

"Is this your assailant?" I ask, facing her.

Fatima stares at Diego a little while longer before looking at her parents and then Sondra.

"No," Fatima whispers as tears fall. "He's too tall. The man was shorter, like me. He also had bigger muscles. The defendant's voice is too deep, even while yelling."

I hand Fatima some more tissue before taking my seat.

"I rest my case, your honor."

"You may return to your seat," Judge Ruby tells Fatima.

From my periphery, I see Sondra swipe her hand over her face before taking her seat also. "I rest, your honor."

Judge Ruby leans back in his chair while organizing the papers on his desk. The officer walks Diego to his seat beside me and remains there.

"In the case of the people versus Diego Sanford, Mr. Sanford is not guilty."

"Thank you, Jesus!" Mrs. Sanford yells before my brain can process the end of the case. "Thank you, Jesus!" she repeats, jumping to her feet.

Diego stands to face her, and she pulls him in for a hug. "Jesus, Jesus, Jesus," she repeats, tears flowing from her eyes.

Smiling, I stand to leave, but she pulls me into the hug as well.

"Thanks for saving my son," she says, before letting us go.

I relax a little, realizing that it was foolish of me to think I wouldn't be able to handle criminal court. Every case may not be like this one, but I enjoyed the thrill of the challenge.

"Thank you, Mr. Campbell," Diego says, extending his hand to me. "We don't have any money to pay you, but I could—"

"It's gratis," I say, giving him my card. "If you have any trouble with the law here on out, or with getting into college, just call me."

I turn to leave but see Fatima crying in her father's arms.

"She has nightmares every time she goes to sleep," her mother scolds me. "She was so close to having closure. Now, she may never heal from this!"

I have no words to offer as I walk away. As a gamer, I understand that every time someone wins, someone else must lose. I pray that they find the man who did this, but putting an innocent man away is not the path to recovery.

"Good job, boss," Cordelia says as I open the door for us to exit.

A faint smile comes across my face. "Thanks. I then look at her growing bump. She's a little over three months, and I can't stop thinking about what I'm going to do when she goes on maternity leave.

"I booked a reservation for you and Dez," Cordelia says, surprising me.

"How did you know about—"

"She called the office and asked which courthouse you were at so she could look up restaurants in the area."

Dez hasn't been back to the office since their little spat, so I'm surprised Cordelia was willing to help her.

"That was nice of you. Which restaurant?"

"Once you turn your phone on, all your questions will be answered. I'll see you tomorrow, boss."

Chapter 12: Justin

May 8, 2015

"Didn't think you were going to make it," I greet Rome as he joins me, his parents, and his grandparents in line to enter Dez's graduation. She only got eight tickets, and the eight of us are the lucky ticket winners. The rest of the family will celebrate with us later today at the graduation party at her parents' house.

"I didn't expect my flight to get delayed."

"You should've come in last night," Pop scolds him.

"Today makes one month since Jane and I have been married. It was...hard leaving her."

Chuckling, I suppress the inappropriate joke that comes to my mind since we are in front of Rome's grandparents.

"I'm sad Jane couldn't make it," Ms. Rose pouts.

"She'll be here in July, Ma. Just wait a little longer," Romeo says as we walk into the stadium.

We quickly take our seats and get comfortable. I've been around Rome and Dez's family so long that even the extended family considered me one of them.

"I wanted Dezzy to come to the house before graduation to take pictures," one of her grandmothers says as we take our seats.

"She probably stayed in the city because it's closer to the stadium," Romeo assumes. "The closer she is to the venue, the closer she is to being on time," he jokes.

Everyone laughs as I take Dez's camera from around me. The ceremony will be starting soon, and I want to make sure I get Dez walking in.

"What're you doing with that?" Rome asks me.

"Dez demanded that I take pictures of her."

"Is that the one you bought?"

"Nah. She says graduation isn't special enough to use the new one."

"Graduation isn't special enough?" Rome chuckles. "What's she waiting for—her wedding day?"

"Beats me," I say, adjusting the setting to compensate for the sunny day.

I'd grown tired of telling Dez to rip the bandage off and use the new camera. If I were a penny pincher, I would've returned the camera by now.

"Do you know what you're doing?" Rome inquires.

"For the most part." In reality, I know exactly what I'm doing. The same way I gave Dez law assessments, was the same way she assessed my photography skills.

"I'll still take some pictures on my phone. You look out of place with that camera, and I'm not about to deal with Dezzy's mouth because no one took decent pictures of her."

"Trust me, the pictures will be great."

Rome laughs. "She probably just taught you what to do in one-sitting. You haven't had any real practice."

I smile. "I've had plenty of practice. You have no idea what..." Rome and I lock eyes, and I sigh. I'm tired of carrying this burden. We've never kept secrets from each other. It's also time for me to rip the bandage off. "Rome, Dez and I have been—" The band begins playing "Pomp and Circumstance," cutting me off.

"Tell me later," Romeo says, taking his phone out.

I face the procession and prepare to record a video. Dez'll be marching in with the College of Arts and by last name, so though I have a little while, I want to be ready.

"Graduations are so boring," I confess.

"You could've only come to the party, and Dezzy would've understood."

I chuckle. Dez would've in fact understood that my love for her had somehow dwindled because how dare I not attend her graduation, especially after her godmother begged for a ticket.

After recording Dez's entrance, I cut the camera off and sit back in my seat until the distribution of degrees. Rome can take all the pics he wants on his phone; I know my shots are the only photos Dez will care about.

***

"Am I trippin', or has GSU's graduation gotten longer since we graduated?" Rome asks as we wait a few blocks away from the stadium for Dez.

Chuckling, I shake my head. "Either it's gotten longer, or we're getting too old to sit through events like this."

Rome chuckles as his mother lets out a sigh of relief. "Finally!" she exclaims as Dez heads our way.

"Hey, graduate!" Pop says, pulling Dez into a hug.

"What took you so long? Your grandparents left," Ms. Rose scolds.

"This is your first time seeing me since getting my degree, and you want to ask what took so long?" Dez asks her mother.

Ms. Rose rolls her eyes before hugging her daughter. "Congratulations, sweetie." She kisses Dez's cheek, and I decide to take a quick picture of Dez and her parents. After the three of them let each other go, Dez turns to Rome and me and opens her arms. Rome returns the gesture, and I prepare to take a picture of the siblings, but when Dez locks eyes with me, I sling her camera over my back.

"I did it!" she says, jumping into my arms. I catch her, wrapping one arm around her waist and using my free hand to play in her hair. She wraps her arms around my neck and legs around my body before kissing me passionately. If kissing like this in front of her parents doesn't bother her, then it doesn't bother me either. Very little bothers me about our relationship since our return from New York.

"You did it," I whisper into her ear when she pulls away. "Congratulations."

She smiles at me before hopping down and walking over to Rome.

"Thanks for coming, big bro," she says, throwing her arms around him. He stands there, scarcely moving.

"What the hell just happened?" he whispers.

Dez looks at me. "Guess you still haven't told him."

I shrug. "He got to the graduation too late."

"Told me what?" Rome asks, clearly pissed.

"Dez and I have been dating since Valentine's Day," I confess.

"She's the chick you've been trying to tell me about?" Rome asks.

"Guess y'all haven't gotten the wedding pictures back yet," Dez jokes, motioning for me to give her the camera.

I face Romeo then. "Every time I tried to tell you about our relationship, you always said you were busy, or you came up with an excuse not to listen."

"Not to listen to how you seduced my sister?" Rome asks, shoving me.

"Calm down, Romeo," I say, shoving him back. He and I have gotten into our share of disagreements, but not once have we ever gotten physical.

"No need to get physical," Dez says, stepping between me and her brother. "I don't want you two to make a big deal out of this; it's my graduation day after all."

I gently move her away. "It's not going to get physical," I state.

"Yo, I need you to explain why you're comfortable kissing my sister like that."

"Do you need glasses, bro? I kissed him," Dez says, reviewing the photos I took.

"I tried to tell you in February that—"

"You ain't try hard enough," Rome argues, still heated.

My patience for Romeo is depleted now. "I didn't try hard enough?" I ask, closing the gap between us. "In February you were heartbroken and didn't care what I had to tell you. You were so selfish when you came in March that you didn't care about anyone but yourself and your case. Your pop dissuaded me from telling you last month. Tell me, Rome, at which point when you were being a self-centered friend was I supposed to share the news with you? Or would you have preferred a text? When's the last time you called just to check on me? Just to ask what I'm up to, or what's going on in my life? Nah, you only call if it pertains to Jane. You've been shitty to all of us, but now you wanna come back and assert dominance? Get outta here."

Rome's face softens as he looks from me to his parents. "Y'all knew?"

"For quite some time now," his mom answers.

"And y'all are okay with it?"

His parents look at each other and chuckle. "Okay with two consenting adults choosing to date?" His mother scoffs.

"Is Justin some kind of criminal that we should know about?" Pop asks.

"No, but he did have his first criminal trial last month," Dez says, standing beside me. "These pictures came out great! I guess you have been paying attention to my lessons."

I shrug. "I don't mean to brag, but I was in the gifted program at school."

Dez laughs as a group of friends call her name.

"I'm finna hang out with them before coming to the condo. You two gonna be alright?" She asks, looking from me to Rome. He's silent, so I take it upon myself to reassure her, though I'm unsure of the answer myself.

"We'll be fine. Text me if you need anything." I kiss her cheek, and she disappears into the crowd.

"I'll see you two at the party," Ms. Rose says as she and Pop turn to leave.

I glance at Romeo, surprised that he isn't leaving with his parents. Previously, Romeo was supposed to come back to the condo with me, but now... "Are you still riding with me?"

Romeo glances in my direction before walking toward the parking deck. I walk apace with him and unlock the doors when we reach the SUV. The ride to my condo is silent, not even the radio plays. There are only silence and traffic. He may have a lot to think about, but I feel relieved, like a weight has been lifted.

***

Romeo gasps and freezes in the hallway when we enter the condo. "What happened to your pad?"

Glancing in his direction, I see him staring at the framed blue and white flower canvas Dez hung in the entryway.

"Oh, that," I say, using the back of my hand to rub my freshly shaven face. "Dez said the place looked like a bachelor pad."

"Because it was a bachelor's pad. Now it looks warm and welcoming, like a home."

I walk to the blue couch and move a gold throw pillow out of my way before sitting.

"Dez asked if she could spruce up the place, and I said sure. Next thing I know, there were floor-length curtains in the living room, floor vases with fake flowers in every corner, and paintings on all the walls."

Rome stops at the bathroom. "Fuzzy rugs, candles, and scented hand soap?" He doubtfully asks before joining me on the couch.

"You should see the bedroom." I reach for the TV remote as the implication of the words I said registers in my mind. From my periphery, I see Rome's frown return.

"What's really going on with you and Dezzy?" He somberly inquires.

Leaning back on the couch, I tell him everything, leaving out the intimate parts. I even share the concerns I have about how far our relationship would go.

"Where is it going?" Romeo asks, his tone gentler now. "You've never wanted to be in a committed relationship before, so what makes Dezzy different?"

"I actually care about her. I couldn't handle her the way I did other women."

"So, you're with her out of guilt?"

"No," I object. "At first I was curious about how far we'd make it, but then Dez showed me the benefits of a monogamous relationship."

"What benefits?" Rome asks, raising an eyebrow.

"Like how encouraging it is to have someone text me on court dates reminding me to do my best and that I'm still great even if the case doesn't end the way I want it to. Having someone there whose voice is enough to assuage the anxious thoughts attempting to flood my mind. How comforting it is to kiss, hold, and wake up to the same woman every day."

"You sound like you love her," Rome scoffs.

"I do love her," I say before we lock eyes. "She's definitely still feisty, but she's also a caring woman who I enjoy spending my time with," I explain, reaching for a PlayStation 4 controller.

Rome grabs the other controller. "I apologize for coming at you the way I did, bro. You're right; I've been a terrible friend to you during the last few months, and you still had my back. Not that you need my input, but I wish you and Dezzy nothing but the best in the future."

"Thanks, man. I wanted to talk to you about this since the day after Valentine's. I really could've used your advice earlier on," I say, going to

Mortal Kombat X.

"Wait, so when I kept calling Valentine's night, and you didn't answer..."
He looks at me while hovering over Takeda in the game.

Clearing my throat, I choose Cassie and start a match. "Dez and I were
still on our date."

Romeo stares at the side of my face, drawing his own conclusions until
round one begins. I win the first match, naturally. Since moving to Brooklyn, Romeo's been slacking on video games the way I've been slacking on
the gym. My winning streak doesn't last long, though. Romeo wins rounds
two and three.

"Dang, bro, are you mad or something?" I ask, scooting to the edge of
the couch as round four begins.

"You told Dezzy we wouldn't get physical, remember?" he snickers. "I'm
just releasing my frustration on the game."

"I hope you got it all out because you aren't winning any more rounds,"
I say, hitting his character with a double-attack combo.

The front door unlocking causes Romeo to pause the game and give me
a baffled look.

"I'm late!" Dez exclaims, running into the living room. She glances between me and Romeo. "Are y'all good?"

"We're good," Rome answers.

Dez lets out a sigh of relief. "Okay, I won't be long. I just have to change
clothes and freshen up my makeup," she says before dashing into the
bedroom.

"You gave her access to your villa?" Rome asks, floored.

I shrug. "She wanted me to stop eating out as much as I did, so she made
dinner for us. That was hard to do on days I got off late, so I gave her a key
to come and go as she pleases."

Rome whistles as he resumes the game. "That's a huge step for you."

I slowly nod. "Things between us are great. I don't see it ending."

"That sounds like marriage," Romeo says, and I pause the game to look at him.

"That's the one thing she and I don't agree on," I admit.

"You're still anti-marriage?"

"I'm not anti-marriage; I'm anti me getting married."

"You're still not over how Alana ended things?" He asks, shaking his head. "You gotta let that go, man. Dezzy isn't going to hang around and play house with you. She wants to get married."

"I know."

"You're going to have to make a decision, Justin. Either let her go or find a black tux; there's no in-between."

"How could you be so optimistic about marriage? You're on your second one," I scoff.

"And I'm as happy as can be."

"That's because you're a helpless romantic," I scoff.

"It's because I know that all women aren't like my ex. Love exists, and I've always wanted to get married and have a family. Just because it didn't work out the first time doesn't mean I should give up."

"Divorces are at an all-time high," I inform.

"Yet people still continue to get married," he argues before chuckling. "If they didn't, then you'd be out of a job."

"All I have to do is touch my face up, and then we can go," Dez says, zooming into the bathroom.

I resume the game while silently thinking about Romeo's words. If he had told me this earlier, then I wouldn't have hesitated about breaking up with Dez. Now that I love her, though? I exhale, and Rome glances at me.

"It's a hard decision to make," I mumble. It would be selfish of me to string her along, but I don't want to lose another woman that I love.

I win the fourth match, but Dez exits the bathroom before Rome and I can start another game.

"Let's go!" she orders. "Can you believe I'm going to be late to my own grad party?" she cries.

"Yes," Romeo and I answer in unison.

"Hurry up. Traffic is pretty bad," Dez says, walking toward the door.

"Should we tell her now that we told her the wrong time for the party?" Romeo asks as we follow Dez's trail.

"Nah. Let her find out when we get there," I say, locking the door behind us.

Dez glares at us. "What are y'all talking about?" she asks through gritted teeth.

"Mom told you the party started thirty minutes earlier than it actually did because she knew you'd be late," Romeo explains while I call the elevator.

Frustrated, Dez screams right before we step onto the elevator.

"Was that necessary?" Romeo asks.

"You know she has to throw a temper tantrum," I say as we descend.

"That's what spoiled brats do," Romeo agrees as the elevator reaches the parking deck.

"Don't talk about me as if I'm not here," Dez whines, folding her arms.

Romeo and I laugh as we head to my SUV. Out of habit, I open the passenger door. Rome gives me a baffled look, and I return the favor. I've never opened the door for him, so I don't understand why he thinks I'm doing it now.

"Get out of my way," Dez says, pushing her brother.

"You're letting her ride shotgun?" Romeo asks, betrayed.

"She's my girl," I say as Dez puts on her seatbelt.

"Yeah, but I'm your boy."

I look between Dez and Romeo before saying, "Yeah, but she's my girl."

Romeo shakes his head before getting in the backseat. Surely, he didn't think I'd put my girl in the backseat, even if it is his sister.

"Did Justin tell you about his first criminal case?" Dez asks Rome as I pull out of the parking space.

"When did that happen?" Rome inquires.

I fill him in on the details as we head to his parents' house. Afterward, he shares the details about the second wedding ceremony he and Jane are having in August. As we get closer to their parents' house, Rome and Dez complain about seeing a set of cousins they don't get along with, while my mind wanders back to what Romeo told me at the condo. Dez laughs after Rome makes a joke about their cousin. I glance at her, thinking there's no way I can take that smile off her face.

Chapter 13: Justin

June 19, 2015

"So, if Juneteenth is about freedom and when we should barbecue, then what's the 4th of July?" Dez asks as I drive the rental car.

"Another day off from work," I answer before we laugh. I'd spent the earlier part of the conversation enlightening Dez on Juneteenth when she asked why my firm is closed today.

"As long as I get to eat barbecue on both days, then I'm fine," Dez nonchalantly responds.

I chuckle while shaking my head; of course, she only cares about food.

"You can get barbecue on both days, but if I had to summarize it, I guess the important thing is that Juneteenth commemorates the day Union troops marched to Galveston, Texas and announced that slavery was over."

Dez nods, but I know her mind is elsewhere. "Was it necessary for us to drive to middle Georgia?" she asks. "What is so special about Warner Robins?"

"You're a little antsy," I note. "The drive is less than two hours."

Dez exhales. "I do have a few things on my mind, but nothing I really want to talk about."

"That's obvious," I tell her. She didn't even want to play games on the ride up here. "A former client of mine rents houses out here. He was kind enough to let me use a house free of charge this weekend."

"It must be nice to receive handouts from clients," she says, glancing in the backseat. "It'll be pretty late by the time the food is ready."

"You got off work late," I point out.

She sighs heavily, and I glance at her. "I don't want to talk about work.

"The good thing is you marinated the meat last night, so all I have to do is throw it on the grill once we get settled," I say, wondering if something happened to her at work. There's never been a topic we were too scared to talk about, even my former sex life and current status were on the chopping block last week.

"I've never seen you cook anything but instant noodles," Dez chuckles. "Why do you think you can grill?"

"I used to grill on the farm in high school. Besides, grilling isn't cooking. It's... grilling."

Dez laughs as I turn into the driveway. "Whatever. If all else fails, we'll just eat veggies and fruits for dinner."

It takes us one trip to get everything out of the car and into the house. While I put coal and lighter fluid in the grill, Dez washes the cooking grate and organizes the food so I can easily grab the chicken legs, salmon, corn, and burgers. Dez plates the fruit and garden salads while I man the flames. We also work together to set up folding tables, trays, and chairs. We spread blankets on the ground, and as the food gets finished, Dez places them on the table and uses cake holders to keep the food insect safe.

"That was a smart idea," I compliment, placing the pitcher of limeade she made on the table next to the gallon of water. "I paid to have the lawn treated and to have insect-repellant torches setup around the yard."

Dez chuckles while shaking her head. "Shouldn't you be used to bugs, country boy?"

"That's different. I can tolerate bugs on the farm, but anywhere else? Nah," I say, shaking my head.

"I think everything is ready," she says, looking around. "Everything except my camera." She then pulls her tripod out and begins recording and taking pictures on her old camera.

Nodding, I go into the house and exit a few moments later with Dez's new camera.

"What are you doing with that?!" she asks, rushing to my side.

"Setting up the camera," I answer, placing it on the tripod that I bought for it.

"But I haven't used it yet," she whines.

"I know. That's been bothering me."

She pokes her bottom lip out before rolling her eyes. "Fine. Move. I'll adjust it to my liking."

"The food is getting cold; we don't have time for you to test out all the new features."

"I'll do what I like," she mumbles.

I pour limeade in a cup before fixing a plate. We have enough food for a small gathering; hopefully that means we won't have to eat out all weekend.

"What are we finna do with two cameras?" she cries.

"Capture two different views."

She groans before running back and forth between both cameras to get her desired scenery.

"Make sure one of them gets a good angle of us," I say, taking a seat.

Dez sighs before abandoning both cameras and fixing a plate for herself. I kiss her cheek as she takes a seat beside me.

"All good?" I ask. She nods before eating some pineapple. "Tomorrow isn't promised, you know. You should use the things you want to enjoy now before you die and someone else gets to enjoy them."

"You're right. I should've used the camera a long time ago." She takes a bite out of the chicken before looking at me. "It's cooked all the way through!" she exclaims.

"I can grill," I smugly remind.

"You might know a little something. Maybe I'll get you a grill for your birthday."

"Maybe then you'll come over more often."

She briefly looks from her food to me. "Have you missed having me over these last few weeks?" she asks before bringing a corn cob to her mouth.

I don't want to make her feel bad for picking up shifts at the restaurant and doing photoshoots around Georgia, but I do miss waking up beside her. "Just a little," I finally answer. "Your parents got you a car for graduation, and you've been on the go ever since."

She chuckles. "Have you adjusted to my absence?"

"Unfortunately," I say before giving my plate my full attention. From my peripheral, I see Dez give me a skeptical look, but I ignore it.

We don't say much else as we eat. Afterward, we clean and pack the remaining food in the refrigerator.

"Wanna watch the sunset?" I ask as we finish the food.

"I didn't realize you were that into nature," she says, wiping her hands on a dish towel.

I shrug, and she leads the way outside. I check the time on my watch before ensuring the cameras are still on and positioned correctly. Dez makes herself comfortable on the blanket, and I join her a short while later.

"This is a nice way to spend our last holiday as boyfriend and girlfriend," I say, propping my head on my arms.

Dez jumps up. "What are you talking about?" she stammers. "Is that what this whole trip was about?"

I face her, still reclined. "There's one issue we still haven't been able to see eye-to-eye on, and by this point, we both know one of us will have to give in or we'll have to go our separate ways."

Her eyes widen. "Is this because we haven't spent as much time together? I've been getting accustomed to living at home again and my new work-load. As soon as—"

"I'm talking about marriage, Dez. It wouldn't be fair of me to ask you to give up your dream of getting married, and you know my feelings on the subject haven't changed."

Dez looks at me, crushed. Her cheeks droop as she tries to figure out what to say next. A firework goes off then; a simple one of stars. I check my watch again before clearing my throat.

"Dez, these past months with you have been better than I could've ever imagined. If someone would've told me that I could experience feelings like this again and have them reciprocated, I would've laughed in their face." Another firework goes off then, and I stand up. She stares at me, still speechless with eyes full of worry. "Dez, you are truly beautiful, inside and out. You're caring, creative, smart, and funny. Thanks for convincing me to take a chance on a relationship with you."

A third firework goes off, and I know I need to hurry up. I take her hands in mine and bring her to her feet. She's still silent, and I repress a chuckle, unable to recall another time she's been so quiet.

"What does the firework say?" I ask her.

"It doesn't say—" A firework goes, and I reach into my pocket as she reads it out loud. "I love you, Desdemona," she whispers before giving me a confused look.

"I do love you, Dez, and now I need you to take a chance on me," I say, getting one knee.

Dez gasps as she covers her mouth. The last set of fireworks goes off, and without looking at it, I read what it says.

"Will you marry me?"

Dez squeals as she jumps up and down with her hands still over her mouth.

"I need a verbal answer for this to work," I tease.

Dez lunges onto me, and I close the box to not lose the ring.

"Yes, I'll marry you!" She throws her arms around my neck. "Yes, yes, yes! Don't you ever scare me like that again!" she orders before kissing all over my face. She stops abruptly and looks into my eyes. "What do you mean take a chance on you?"

I caress her cheek. "Will you believe that I'll put away my doubts and fears about marriage so that I can put my best foot forward with you? Will you believe that I'll give our marriage all that I have, remain loyal, and cherish you like the gem you are?"

"Of course, I will, Justin!" She kisses me again.

"Think you can put on the ring that took me hours to pick out?" I ask in between kisses.

Dez laughs while letting me go. After taking the ring out the box, I put it on her finger and listen to her squeal again.

"Wait," Dez says, running over to her old camera, "was this your plan all along?"

She stops the recording and replays the footage, not waiting for me to answer. Chuckling, I grab the new camera, stop the recording, and hand it to her.

"Two different angles; you're so smart, Justin! What a great way to announce our engagement. I just need to edit the footage and splice the videos together. Of course, I'd have to go back and forth so I could get the different angles. Oh, and when I hugged you—"

"You call that a hug? More like a tackle."

Chuckling, Dez rolls her eyes before turning the old camera off and looking at the video on the new one. I take the camera from her and put it to the side before lying down and pulling her on top of me.

"Take a deep breath," I say, playing in her hair with one hand and rubbing her pack with the other. "Let's enjoy this moment. We have all weekend to share the news with everyone; let's just celebrate alone for now."

She raises up and looks at me. "Though I've been feigning for another Valentine's special, I'm not desperate enough to do it out here."

I laugh out loud then. "I'm not talking about making love, Dez," I say, looking into her eyes and caressing her butt.

"I am," she pouts.

I chuckle. "We both can wait for marriage like we originally planned."

She sticks her bottom lip out, and I smile before taking it in my mouth. I'm still apprehensive about our next season, but I'm optimistic. Hopefully, with prayer and work, we'll have the best marriage possible.

Chapter 14: Dezzy

June 23, 2015

I use my fork to roll the leftover grape tomatoes from my garden salad around my plate. My family's mirthful conversation is idle chatter to me. Justin and I are having dinner at my parents' house because Jane and Romeo are in town sightseeing for a week. We're all gathered around the black, rectangular dining room table. I'm sure it's just as surprised as I am that it's being used, but with Jane's addition to the family, the kitchen just won't hold us.

"I'm just not a fan of pound cake," Jane says, shaking her head as she gives Romeo her blue square dessert plate.

"I've never met anyone who's had Rose's pound cake and didn't like it," Dad says.

Jane shrugs. "I've had a dozen slices of pound cake over my life, and they're all just not sweet enough for me. It's like cornbread: no matter who's I try, I still don't like it."

Everyone at the table aside from me gasps. "Check your girl, Rome," Justin says, shaking his head, "before she loses her Black card."

"I took that from her when we went to American Deli earlier, and she ordered barbecue wings with an iced tea."

Even I look at her in shock now.

"She did what?" Dad asks.

"I'm a bona fide Brooklyn girl. Y'all don't remember going to the Chinese store and getting barbecue wings or rib tips with French fries or fried rice?" Jane asks, chuckling.

Mom nostalgically exhales. "I do, and I used to get an iced tea Arizona."

"Case in point," Jane says, pointing to Mom.

Dad shakes his head before grabbing Mom's plate and standing up. "Romeo, I still think you and Jane should spend your vacation here instead of paying for a hotel. There's plenty of room."

I take Justin's plate before standing to go to the kitchen too. Romeo and Jane smile at each other rather than responding.

"They're newlyweds, Gary. They haven't learned to be quiet yet, so they want some privacy," Mom informs.

Jane covers her face, a failed attempt at hiding how red she's turning. Romeo awkwardly stands up, grabs their dishes, and beats everyone to the kitchen. Justin laughs as he heads down the hall. I don't even look in his direction, and Jane notices.

"I'll take those from you," Mom says, grabbing the dishes I've yet to deliver to the kitchen.

"I better run to the bathroom before we leave," Jane says, standing up and going down the hall.

I silently follow behind. She stops at the bathroom door, noticing the light coming from under it.

"Justin's probably going to be a while. Why don't you use the one in my room?" I offer.

Jane looks at me, surprised. "I didn't know you had an en suite," she tells me.

I motion for her to follow me. It is only her second time at my parents' house, let alone Georgia, so of course she didn't know. I open the door, and the faint aroma of the dying raspberry plug-in that I need to change greets us. Jane scrutinizes my room, but her poker face doesn't give me any hints as to what she thinks. Pink fuzzy rugs cover the champagne-colored carpet. A lavender recliner that I begged my parents to buy me in middle school is diagonal to my queen-sized bed. Posters of my favorite princesses and singers hang throughout, and teddy bears on the beanbag that I took from Rome's room when he went to college complete my girlish decor.

"The bathroom's to the right of the dresser," I instruct Jane.

She nods before heading into it. I grab my brush from the dresser and look at my reflection as I slide the bristles through my knot-free hair. It's been a while since I've gotten a haircut. My hair has gotten so long that the ends cup my cheek; I haven't had it this long in years.

"You wanna talk about what's been bugging you?" Jane asks before flushing the toilet.

"What do you mean? I'm fine," I lie, dropping the brush. Truth is, I haven't felt like myself since Justin and I got back from Warner Robins.

"You've been quiet and poised all night. No bantering, hitting, or teasing; something's wrong with you."

I don't do any of those with Jane, so she's obviously talking about my interactions with Romeo and Justin. She turns off the faucet and rips a sheet of paper towel before joining me in the room.

"How does Romeo feel about my engagement?"

Sunday afternoon, before Justin and I left Warner Robins, I uploaded our engagement video to my social media account. I sent a message in the family group chat instructing everyone to look at my profile, and within minutes, my phone began blowing up. Justin shared the video on his profile, causing his phone to receive the same consequence. I edited the video to show Justin and I grilling, setting up the backyard, and finally, him proposing. I cropped out the earlier part of the proposal where I was going to cry because I thought he was breaking up with me but kept the fireworks and him asking declaring his love for me. Everyone sent their congratulations, but Rome didn't send a message until later that night.

"Bold of Justin to propose a few days before we arrived, but Romeo will be fine. He came home last month, claiming to be torn between being happy for y'all and pissed. I asked if he loved you; he said yes. I asked if he loved Justin; he said yes. Then I asked if it's really that bad that you two saw in each other what he saw in y'all and fell in love. He sighed and answered no. I told him that it's not a matter of approving your relationship but supporting two people he really cares about."

I nod, glad Romeo is finally coming around. He's going to be the best man after all, so he can't be a sourpuss.

"The question is do you approve?" Jane asks, looking into my eyes. "Do you have doubts or reservations about marrying Justin?"

Exhaling, I sit on the bed. Jane sits on the recliner and folds her arms as she waits for a response.

"I love Justin, and I was thrilled when he proposed, but... maybe I'm getting in over my head."

"You don't think you'll be a good wife?"

I roll my eyes. "I'm not worried about that; Justin and I can talk and figure out spousal roles as our relationship grows."

"Then what's the issue?"

"Justin has lived a full life. He's experienced things I haven't and some things I probably never will."

"You knew that before y'all started dating."

"He's been with a variety of women before me, but they all had one thing in common," I say, glancing at the glow in the dark stars that refuse to come off my ceiling after almost two decades. "All of those women were older, settled in life and their careers. They were doing what they wanted, or they at least knew how to get to the path they wanted to take. Some have even had the same experiences he's had." I scoff before looking at my reflection in the dresser mirror. "I can't even get a call back for an interview. I've been so caught up in my fantasy coming true, that I didn't realize that I may be underqualified to be with Justin. I've never lived on my own or gone on trips so scandalous that I couldn't breathe a word of it upon my arrival back home. There's so much I haven't done yet, and what if one day Justin realizes this and wants someone else because a woman like me doesn't fit the cut?"

Jane stares at me, just as surprised at my candidness as I am. If she's as caring and insightful as Romeo proclaims, however, she'll offer something to pacify my anxieties. I wouldn't dare bring this up to my friends because all of them except Nancy are single, not to mention, they're all my age, so they probably wouldn't have much advice to offer. Jane's older, so she'll definitely know what to say.

"I don't know, Dezzy."

I look at her, dumbfounded.

"What do you mean you don't know?" I nearly yell. "How could you not know?"

"This is only my third time meeting you and Justin. We don't talk enough for me to provide specific answers." Jane walks toward me then. "Even if I did know y'all more, Justin should be the one answering your questions. I'll tell you this though, those other women might be older and more mature, but Justin still didn't care about them enough to give them more than one date. He chose you, Dezzy, to enter a committed relationship with. He decided you were the one worth changing his ways for. That has to be enough for you, but if it isn't, then you have to talk to him."

I roll my eyes and look away from her. "So, you didn't have any fears about marrying Romeo?" I ask, hoping to knock her off her high horse.

Jane scoffs. "Are you kiddin' me? The man reconciles our relationship, proposes, and demands that I marry him within one week! You don't think that was terrifying?" She laughs and sits beside me. "Romeo had the option to move on with his life and never look my way again. Instead, he sought me out and asked for a second chance. That was good enough for me. He showed me his true colors, and I'm choosing to believe it. It's only been two months, but we've been good ever since. You're going to have to talk to your fiancé, address your doubts, and trust that you're making the right decision. Pray and ask God to help you if you're struggling. You don't want to go into your marriage thinking it'll fail."

"Is this where you've been?" Romeo asks Jane, barging into my room with Justin on his heels.

"Gotta keep you two separated before y'all run off and get another tattoo," Justin jokes.

"C'mon, bae, we have a long day tomorrow," Romeo says, stretching his hand toward Jane. She takes it and hops off the bed. She faces me before they exit.

"Text me," she instructs before they leave. The front door opens and closes a few moments later, and I hear their rental car start and pull out of the driveway.

"Are you ready to go, or do you want to crash here tonight?" Justin asks, approaching me.

After graduation, I officially moved back in with my parents, only spending one or two nights a week with Justin. I've slept at the condo every night since our engagement, however.

"Do you think you'll make a good husband?" I ask him.

He gives me a perplexed look. "I can't see much of a difference between what I do now and what I'll do as a husband. As long as you're with me, I'll take care of your needs and wants, mentally," he says, kissing my forehead. "Emotionally." He kisses my lips. "Physically." He kisses my neck.

"You don't think I'll outgrow you?"

Moving away, he gives me an apprehensive look. "What're you talking about, Dez?"

I sigh. "I'm worried about being underqualified to be your wife, and I'm trying not to think that you'll want someone else," I say faster than Buster Rhymes rapping on "Look at Me Now."

Justin's face softens, and he sits beside me on the bed. Of course he was worried. He'd recently proposed—a feat he spent almost twenty years telling himself that he'd never do. Obviously, he was worried that I was having doubts about being with him, not the other way around.

"Where is this coming from, Dez? Why would I outgrow you or look for someone else?"

"Because you're an accomplished lawyer whose future is brightly lit, and I'm a waitress whose only way of living her life's dream is by accepting photoshoot bookings as long as the client is comfortable being outdoors."

"Dez, it's only been one month since you've graduated."

"And in that month, I've learned that I should've remained a business major. That was a promising degree with endless career choices."

"Dez, a week before my undergrad graduation, I got a rejection letter from the law school of my dreams," he shares, looking into my eyes. "The day after me and Rome's grad party, I got a message from Alana congratulating me and inviting me to her wedding. While writing my best man's speech for Rome's first wedding, I got a notification that my financial aid wasn't going to be enough for law school, and I'd have to look into getting some loans. Two weeks before I started law school, I had to move into your parents' house because my housing fell through."

I stare at him, flabbergasted. I didn't know about any of that, especially why he moved in. I thought he did to help my parents' cope with Romeo's absence.

"The season between graduation and figuring out what to do next is hard and scary for almost everyone. Even people who have everything figured out are thrown a sledgehammer to slow them down. It's only been one month since you've graduated; give yourself the space to celebrate that. You changed majors and graduated with honors while everyone else was side-eyeing you; celebrate that. You launched your LLC, and you finally got a car; bask in that. Why do you think you'd be underqualified? Because you haven't set sail in your career yet? Pfft."

"That, and because I'm still figuring out who I am while you already know who you are."

Justin laughs in my face. "Are you serious?" He asks, catching his breath. "Just four months ago I was telling your brother that I'd never be caught dead cooking for a broad. Now look at me, planning a wedding when I never thought I'd get married with a woman I definitely would've never thought I'd be with. People change and grow as they mature through life, and we'll do the same."

"You didn't cook for some broad," I say, pushing him. "You grilled for the love of your life."

"There's a fine line between the two," he teases, and I push him again. He holds me this time, with my back to his chest.

"You overcame your challenges, though. You did what you had to and found a job after graduating law school. I don't know what I'm doing wrong."

"I didn't find a job, Dez. I created a job for myself. I applied to a few places after law school, but I always knew I wanted to work for myself. By the time I finally heard back from a law firm, I was signing the lease for my current building, with some payment assistance from my parents, of course. Dez, things in life don't come easy. You have to work for what you want, and you have to be aware that you aren't the only one competing for the jobs you're applying to. You're spoiled, but you weren't raised with a silver spoon in your mouth, so why do you think life is going to hand you everything you want?"

"I know it's not going to be easy, but I didn't think I'd have to wait this long to get into my field."

"It's been one month, Dez. You cannot microwave your career like a TV dinner. You've worked hard for five years; take this summer to relax. Stop putting in applications and focus on your craft. Keep working at Groove's if you want but also make time to hang out with your friends and family. You deserve to. It's not like you have any bills to pay," he says before chuckling.

I hit his chest with my head before smiling. I'm sure my mental health is begging for some time off.

"I could spend time planning our wedding," I say, caressing his arm.

He exhales then. "Planning a wedding and preparing for Cordelia to take maternity leave," he says, exhaling again. "I'm finna need the peace that passes all understanding to make it through this year."

"I can help alleviate some stress," I say, turning to kiss him.

Mom giggling loudly stops me in my tracks. Justin and I give each other a skeptical look while silently listening.

"That tickles," Mom says, and Justin and I jump off the bed.

"Guess we're going to the condo tonight," Justin says, leading me to the hallway.

"Yep. I think they've realized they don't have to be quiet anymore."

Chapter 15: Justin

July 2, 2015

I gently fend off the hen who is attacking me because I'm stealing her eggs. I've always hated this job, but Momma wants to make a big breakfast for Dez's first Missouri visit. Biscuits, pancakes, and omelets all have one thing in common: these brown eggs I'm stealing. After robbing the six eggs, I move onto the next hen's nest to do the same. This hen is less aggressive, perhaps because she's accepted the nature of things on my parents' farm.

Once the basket is full, I walk across the field to the house with only one floodlight as my guide. I don't need the light, of course. I know every inch of this farm blindfolded.

"Finally," Momma says when I enter. "Give me that basket," she orders, taking it from me before I can offer it.

"What's the rush? Dez is probably still tossing in bed," I say, sitting at the breakfast table in the farmhouse-styled kitchen.

"That's not the point. I'd like to have everything ready for when she wakes up."

"What if the food is cold by the time she wakes up?" I tease.

"If she's not down by the time I'm finished, then I'll send you to get her."

I raise an eyebrow, surprised. "She and I aren't allowed to share a room until we're married, but you're giving me permission to wake her from her slumber?"

Momma glares at me, and Dad playfully hits my back. "Give your mother a break. You nearly gave her a heart attack when you announced your engagement, and that it was to Dezzy of all people. After years of accepting that you'd never get married, she's had less than a month to comprehend that she's going to be a mother-in-law."

"Mother-in-law?" Momma scoffs. "Grandmother."

"Whoa," I say, grabbing an orange from the fruit bowl in front of me. "We're holding off on kids for as long as we can."

Momma throws her hands up in defeat before grabbing some eggs and cracking them into a large glass bowl. I chuckle softly; I love messing with Momma. I think she knows that too, which is why she always follows up on my shenanigans. The kid part is true, though. Neither of us feels ready enough for children, let alone has a desire.

"There is no way in the world that people do this every single day of their lives," Dez croaks as she enters the kitchen. My parents and I laugh as a rooster crows. "And that awful sound! I thought it was something movies added to be dramatic, but no. This is real. The rooster is real. It's minutes after six, and that bird is screaming at the top of his lungs."

"Good morning to you too, Dezzy," Dad says.

"Interesting to see that you've hardly changed," Momma says, amused.

Dez and I got in late last night, so my parents didn't get to welcome us. Dez and my parents have met a handful of times, thanks to them visiting when I was in undergrad and law school. They didn't know we were even dating, so when they saw our engagement video, I spent an hour on the phone explaining that it was not a prank and that Romeo, and I are still friends. Dez walks to the table and stands in front of me. She's wearing overalls with a red, long-sleeved plaid shirt underneath. Her hair, which she surprisingly still hasn't cut, is parted down the middle with two braids on each side with two small red bows at the end. She looks really cute.

"How are you not tired?" Dez asks, stealing a few orange slices from me.

I shrug. "I think my body is programmed to wake up at five whenever I'm on the farm."

"Whenever you're home," Momma corrects.

"Atlanta is home," Dez and I say.

Dad laughs as Momma goes on a thousand-word-per-minute rant about not forsaking my roots. I'll never be ashamed of being from Missouri or being raised on a farm. I never had to drop out of school to help out, thankfully, and my parents made enough to support me through college. Their farm is still successful now. They supply local grocery stores with fresh and chemical-free vegetables and fruits.

"Justin, show Dezzy around the farm, and by the time y'all get back, I should be finished with breakfast."

"I'd rather wait until it's brighter to have a tour."

My parents and I glance at each other before laughing. "Momma's being polite, babe. She actually wants us to do a couple of chores and get out of her hair," I translate, standing up and leading Dez out the backdoor. "My parents are thrilled that you're here, though."

"So thrilled that they send me out to work?" she asks as the sun rises.

"You'll be here for a few days, and they want you to be comfortable. Didn't you also say you wanted to see me in all my country boy glory?" I joke as I lead her to the cow stalls.

"I guess," she mumbles.

"I've never seen you so cranky," I admit, grabbing two buckets.

"We got in late and are up early. If you want a pocket of sunshine, try waking me after eight."

"This should wake you up," I say, placing a stool beside the first cow. "Have you ever milked a cow?"

"No," she says, scrunching up her face. "When would I even have the opportunity? Where are the gloves?"

I chuckle as I look around for a pair of gloves the farmhands may have left around. "I usually ditch the gloves, but I'll grab a pair."

She sits on the stool as I walk to the shed a few feet away. As I'm walking back to Dez with the pair that I found, I see her petting and talking to the cow. Something about running away to a magical place where they could sleep to their heart's content. I show her how to milk the cow and assure her that it brings the cow no pain. After storing the milk, I demonstrate how to feed and water the animals. She wakes up and becomes more energetic with the more chores we complete.

"What's the purpose of having this beautiful red barn if y'all just let the animals run around the field?"

"The animals have an enclosed section," I correct. "They'd eat all the produce if we allowed them on this side. The barn is where we used to house the animals. However, I bought a lot of land for my parents and hired workers to build stables and pens. Then, I had the barn renovated, and now we use it for gatherings."

"You bought your parents a lot of land?" she asks, surprised.

I bashfully look away. "The land has been an eyesore for years. A house was destroyed by a fire, and the owners moved. No one showed interest in it, so I got it for a good deal. That way my parents could have more room."

"How could a sweet and caring man like you ever be a womanizer?" Dez asks as we approach the barn.

Ignoring her, I open the barn, and we step inside.

"This is magnificent!" she praises. "Concrete floors, picturesque windows, and an iron wrought chandelier." She faces me, and I can tell she's scheming. "Justin," she says, taking hold of my hand, "let's have our wedding here."

"Our wedding *here*? In a barn on the farm that I grew up on? Nope." I walk out, leaving her to follow.

"C'mon, babe," she says, running after me. "Why not?"

"The whole town will turn out, and my parents don't have the heart to tell anyone no," I say, taking her under my arm. "There are plenty of farmhouse venues in Georgia. Let's go back to the house, and I'll pull up some on my laptop."

"You don't want your hometown to know you're married?" Dez asks as we walk through the kitchen's backdoor.

"I don't care who knows I'm married."

"Then why don't you want to have the wedding here?"

My parents look at us. "Your wedding?" Momma asks.

"Yes. Justin showed me the barn, and I think it'll be perfect. I see a makeshift aisle with tables on both sides. On tables are centerpieces with candles." Dez stops and looks at all of us. "Battery-operated candles."

"The fall foliage on the farm is to die for," Momma shares.

"Why are y'all teaming up?" I groan. "Help me out, Dad."

Dad shakes his head. "It's actually profitable, son. You'll save money booking with me and your momma."

"You're charging me?" I ask before my parents laugh.

"You think we'll let you use the barn as a venue free of charge just because you paid to have the barn and house renovated?" Dad asks.

Dez stares at me, mouth wide open, and I glare at Dad. "No one is supposed to know that."

"You're about to get married, son. The only secrets you should keep from your wife are parties, flowers, and gifts."

Sighing, I look at Dez. I can't read her expression, though. I prefer the gifts and donations I give to remain in the dark. I don't need public recognition for anything; such sentiments make me uncomfortable. Buying land and paying for renovations is chump change compared to the investments my parents made in me.

"Why don't you want to get married here, Justin?" Dez asks, walking over to me. "Does it have to do with—"

"It has nothing to do with Alana," I say, taking Dez's hands in mine. "This is my home away from home. Here, I'm not a big-notch divorce lawyer who lives in a fancy condo. I'm Justin, the farmers' kid. If a big fiasco is to be made, then I'd rather that be done somewhere else."

"What if I promise to keep it simple?"

I raise an eyebrow. "Simple like your high school grad party?"

Chuckling, she shakes her head. "Nope. Only family and very closest friends. We'll do elegant instead of gaudy."

"We may also come down on the price if that helps," Momma chimes in. Dez and I laugh.

"What about all of your bells and whistles?" I ask Dez.

She smirks. "I'll save that for the engagement party, which will be in Georgia, apparently."

I smile. "I guess it's a good bargain." I lean in to kiss her, but I'm met with emptiness as she turns to face my mother.

"Tell me more about the foliage. How cold will it be in a few months? I didn't smell anything foul; is that because y'all keep the animals on the lot on the other side of the property? You think we'll smell anything in the barn?" Dez asks, rapidly firing questions.

My mother is no better, answering just as fast and quickly as Dez throws questions out.

"Are you following?" Dad asks, standing beside me.

I chuckle. "I can understand my woman; can you understand yours?"

Chuckling, Dad hits my back. "You think I remained happily married for over three decades because I don't understand my wife?"

Chapter 16: Justin

October 17, 2015

"Bro, nervous is not even the word to describe how I feel right now. I'm shaking in my boots," I confess to Romeo.

We're getting dressed in my bedroom at my parents' house. The groomsmen are a few doors down getting dressed, leaving me and my best man to have one last conversation before the ceremony starts.

He laughs. "You're not wearing boots."

I give him an exasperated look before resuming buttoning my lavender dress shirt. "Why in the world am I this scared?"

Rome shrugs. "I don't know what's scarier: the fact that you're getting married or the fact that you're marrying Dezzy."

I side-eye him, and he hits me playfully. "She's a handful, bro, but I guess that's what you need." He begins fixing my baby blue bowtie then. "It's natural to feel nervous, but this is supposed to be the happiest day of your life."

"I thought that was only for the chicks," I say, moving away. "Tell me I'm not making a mistake and that I have nothing to worry about," I demand, making eye contact.

Rome chuckles while shaking his head. "Man, you got it bad. You're asking a man who got married twice for advice?"

I chuckle then, relaxing a little. "I really need my brother today, all jokes aside."

"All jokes aside, you have nothing to worry about. It should be the happiest day of your life too, or at least one of the happiest days. You're marrying the woman you love."

I examine his face for any hints of anger or disdain. None exist, though. Rome really did change after our talk on Dez's graduation day. He's returned to being the good friend he's always been. He planned my bachelor party, made sure the groomsmen had their attire in a timely fashion, and ensured his parents and our wedding party arrived on time. That selfish man he temporarily has vanished. He doesn't even seem bothered by me being with his sister anymore.

"You've gotta keep a cool head, bro. Had Jane not told me she was nervous on our wedding day, I never would've known. She entered so gracefully and beautifully that I was convinced that she was confident in our decision to be married quickly. She told me she was trembling." Rome smiles and shakes his head. "Her father had to hold her tightly. The only thing that calmed her down, though, was seeing me at the altar smiling at her."

"That's crazy because you were a mess," I say before we laugh.

"She didn't see that though. She saw her groom eagerly waiting for her, and that was enough to relax. You got this, Justin. Your bride is counting on you."

I stare at him, speechless. He sighs and pulls me in for a hug. "You better get your act together; that's my sister you'll be taking care of. You know she's spoiled, so she's used to having her own way."

I chuckle; there's the Rome I know.

There's a knock at the door before it opens. "It's time," Dad says. "Let's get it."

Dad, like Romeo, looks spiffy in the purple tuxedo and baby blue shirt. Dez demanded that I wear the inverted colors. I agreed, eager to wear anything but white; I'm too messy for that. I grab my baby blue tux jacket and head down the hall.

***

Glancing in, I can barely recognize the barn. The decorating company my parents hired did a fantastic job transforming it from an unused building to an incredible wedding venue. Stringed lights and lanterns hang from the ceiling. Circular tables with white tablecloths and jeweled candle center-pieces stand on either side of the long, sparkly, floor runner rug. The rug stops in front of a raised stage. There's the pastor's podium, the small table where Dez and I will light unity candles, and floor vases with real flowers and other plants.

The DJ, a girl I went to high school with, has her sound system set up and is on the stage placing microphones in the stands. After the ceremony and a few pictures, the stage will be broken down and turned into a dance floor. Looking up, I see the projector screen that will play the slideshow of pictures Dez handpicked for today. Pictures of us together as kids and with friends and family. Taking a deep breath, I shut the barn door.

"No turning back now," my cousin says, hitting my back as the other groomsmen trail behind him.

"I guess falling off that tractor and breaking your arm didn't stunt your strength," I joke.

He snickers. "Heck, naw. You think I'd be the quarterback of my college team if it did?"

"The way he and Dez couldn't take their eyes off each other last night at dinner prove they ain't thinkin' about turnin' back now," Dez's cousin states.

"Unless it's to the hotel down the street," my cousin teases.

While laughing, I look at Rome, who wears a smile instead of joining in on our boyish jokes. As an only child, I can't fathom how awkward it must be for someone whose sibling and best friend are marrying each other, but I'm glad he's decided to be a good sport rather than a party pooper. The bridesmaids join us. They're wearing lavender just like the groomsmen.

"Where's Jane?" Rome asks Cindy, concerned.

Cindy, Dez's best friend and maid of honor, exhales deeply as she takes in how handsome Rome looks. I smirk; she better not let Jane catch her doing that.

"Dezzy said she wanted to be alone with her matron of honor or something," Cindy answers. "I'm not sure what it's about."

"What you tell me, bro? Relax?" I ask Romeo, patting his back.

"Everyone, line up," the wedding planner orders. The rest of the party joins us, and we all get in the order we'd practiced yesterday.

Kenny Lattimore's "For You" begins, and my parents enter the barn as soon as the doormen open the doors. Dez's mother and uncle are next, followed by me and Romeo.

"How you feel, man?" he asks as we walk.

Everyone is looking at us. Childhood friends from both sides, schoolmates, and family members were surprised either by the fact that I'm tying the knot or that Dez is getting married so young. Even Cordelia and her family show up. I take a deep breath and remember why I'm here.

"I feel good, bro," I finally answer as we approach the stage.

I see our parents sitting on the front row as Rome and I walk up the steps to the right of the stage. My childhood pastor nods his head at me before looking forward. I do the same and observe the wedding party entering. There's a noticeable emptiness after Cindy takes her place at the foot of the stage with the rest of the bridesmaids. I glance at Rome, who is trying not to worry. Just as everyone begins whispering, Jane enters. Romeo lets out a sigh of relief, and I see her wink at him before looking at me. She chuckles before walking to and ascending the staircase on the left.

"Please stand for the entrance of the bride," the pastor says.

Everyone stands, and I nervously rock from left to right. Momma silently scolds me, causing me to stop. Sabrina, my cousin, begins singing Whitney Houston's "I Believe in You and Me." The flower girls, Sabrina's twin daughters, enter, throwing white petals as they walk.

Dez enters on her father's arm a few moments later, and I gasp. She's breathtakingly beautiful. She's wearing a strapless, sparkly baby blue ball-gown. Even Cinderella would be jealous. She really wanted to cut her hair and wear it in finger waves, whatever that is, but her mother begged her not to, so she cut her hair to just under her cheeks. It's styled with a side part and curls; a floral hair clip finishes her look.

"Breathe, bro," Romeo whispers to me before chuckling.

I need to blink, but I don't want to take my eyes off her. The song's lyrics minister to me then. Dez was adamant about this song playing as she walked down the aisle, and now I realize it's her declaration of faith in our marriage. We lock eyes as she gets closer, and she smiles at me. It's no longer that uncertain smile she gave me on Valentine's Day, but a confident one, ensuring she does in fact believe in us. I smile back, hoping to let her know I'm ready to enter this new season with her.

Her father walks her up the steps and stops in front of the pastor.

"Ladies and gentlemen, you may be seated. We are gathered here today to commemorate the marriage of Justin Tyriek Campbell to Desdemona Hana Raymond."

Dez smirks at the announcement of my middle name, and I chuckle at the sour face she makes when she hears her full first name.

"Who gives this woman away?" the pastor asks.

"I do," Dez's father says, before looking at his daughter with tears in his eyes.

Dez rolls her eyes. "You said you wouldn't cry, Daddy," she sighs, hugging him.

He kisses her cheek before taking her hand and putting it in mine. He looks into my eyes but says nothing. Probably because he told me everything he felt a few days ago. Dez is his baby, and it may be his fault she's spoiled, but she takes care of the people who take care of her. I reminded him that I'm no stranger to Dez or to how much he's spoiled her.

Mr. Raymond smiles at me, then at Romeo behind me, and then walks down the steps to sit beside his wife.

Dez and I lock eyes then, smiling while holding each other's hands.

"You're the most handsome man here," she announces before everyone laughs. "My bad; didn't expect the mic to catch that."

"I have to be since I'm marrying the most beautiful woman on the planet," I respond.

"Second most," Romeo coughs, causing the audience to laugh again.

"Either you can't count, or you can't see," Dez rebuttals, causing me to laugh.

The pastor clears his throat and begins the ceremony. He talks about the importance of unity and love before praying and instructing Dez and I to light the unity candles. Afterward, he calls for the rings, and Romeo and Jane present them. He prays over them before leading Dez and me into the ring vows and traditional wedding vows.

"I now pronounce you Mr. and Mrs. Campbell; Justin, you may kiss your bride."

Dez hands her bouquet to Jane before smiling at me bashfully. I laugh to myself, thinking it's too late for her to be shy. Placing one hand on her waist and one in her hair, I dip and kiss her. She wraps her hands around my neck and head as our guests clap and cheer.

We smile at each other after parting, and we descend the steps and head out of the barn with the wedding party following behind. Dez was right about having the wedding in the fall. The colors on my parents' farm made for the perfect backdrop. The photography company that Dez put through the ringer before hiring directed all of us on where and how to pose. Dez is either too ecstatic about our wedding or finally trusts them enough to not criticize what they're doing. After what seems like forever, according to how tired my facial muscles are from smiling, we're permitted access to the barn once again.

***

"What was the hold-up with you and Jane anyway?" I ask Dez, stepping out of the shower.

We checked into the hotel almost an hour ago and have been sharing wedding day stories with each other all night. The conversation didn't end when she got in the shower earlier, and it doesn't stop now.

"I was getting some last-minute sisterly advice."

"Like what?" I inquire, moisturizing my face and lips.

"The usual stuff," she answers as I begin drying off. "How to overcome last-minute jitters, how to ignore everyone staring at me, and of course, one of the most important things."

"What's that?" I ask, rinsing with mouthwash.

"The best kind of lingerie to wear the first night."

I spit the mouthwash out before peeking into the bedroom. Smirking, Dez sits up in bed with her robe closed but untied.

"Jane said to keep it simple because grooms are usually too focused on their *wives* to notice what she's wearing."

"What did you decide on?" I ask, approaching her.

"I kept it a tad simple," she says, taking off the robe, revealing a white lace bra and panty set.

I lick my lips while tossing the robe onto the nearby recliner, causing her to chuckle. I admire her in the soft light coming from the bed's headboard. Dez bites her bottom lip, showing she's just as enamored with me. I kiss her, slowly and passionately. She pulls me on top of her as she lies down. I kiss her from her neck to her breasts to her abs and to her waist before going to her outer left thigh. I gaze at her beautiful water lily tattoo before slowly kissing and biting it. The lavender flower sits on green lily pads with drops of water dew.

"You have another one to kiss," she softly reminds, caressing my head.

"I'm saving that one for later." I kiss her inner thigh before meeting her stare.

Dez chuckles, and I continue kissing her while beginning to undress her. Dez hands me a condom before I can stuff my face. Taking it, I frown.

"Don't I get a taste first?" I ask.

She shakes her head. "You've been depriving me for over eight months." She raises my head so we can look into each other's eyes. "I want you now, baby."

Smirking, I stand up, strip, and put on the condom. We definitely don't want kids anytime soon. Dez isn't a fan of birth control, so this is our best choice, but as we lock eyes, we both know that condoms won't be used for long.

"I want my dessert tomorrow," I demand, lying on top of her.

Dez kisses my lips. "Whatever you want. Just give me what I've been missing."

I chuckle, shaking my head at how spoiled she is.

"Yes, ma'am," I say, unhooking her bra and burying my face.

Chapter 17: Dezzy

February 14, 2016

"Dinner was great, babe," I tell Justin as we hold hands and walk around downtown Atlanta.

Laughs and loud chatter surround us from nearby couples celebrating Valentine's Day. The trees we pass are strung with red, pink, and purple LED lights.

"Did you like the accompanying orchestra?" Justin asks.

"Definitely. Live R&B music is top tier."

Justin pulls me closer to him then. "I have one more place to take you."

"I remember where you took me after dinner last year," I tease. He chuckles but remains silent as we continue walking.

If our first date last year was a fairytale, then the last four months of marriage have been happily ever after. I'd never lived on my own, so I didn't have much adjusting to do when I moved into the condo. Justin, on the other hand, had spent years living alone, and some days, he literally showcased it. Like when I walked into the bathroom right after he got out of the shower, and he thought I was an intruder. He's gotten better, though, and he never makes me feel like he doesn't want me to be there.

Career-wise, Justin has been taking on more criminal cases, often picking up clients who can't afford attorneys. He has since accepted the fact that all cases aren't black and white, causing him to keep it real with his clients, informing them of possible consequences if found guilty.

I have yet to hear back from any company, making me feel like my degree is useless. Though Justin said I don't have to, I've continued working at Groove's just to not go crazy from sheer boredom. I've even begrudgingly flirted with getting an MBA.

"Here we are," Justin says, stopping in front of a one-story, glass-front building.

We're unable to see in, despite the glass. Justin unlocks the door and motions for me to enter. I only take two steps in before Justin joins me and flips on the light.

"This would be the reception area," he informs us, gesturing to the empty room before us. The floor is white marble, and the walls are painted egg white. "The first bathroom is through that hallway on the left."

"Nice. I see a lot of potential. Are you thinking about moving your office here?"

"Nah, babe. This is yours," Justin says, placing the key in my hand.

"What?" I breathlessly ask.

"Most of the paperwork is complete; the last thing is your name on the deed. After all, this is going to be your photography studio."

My eyes swell with tears as I face him. "Why, Justin?" I mumble, unable to get rid of the lump in my throat.

"How do you think it looks for my wife to be working at Groove's simply because she's bored and waiting until it's warm again to restart her business?"

I choke out a scoff. "You got this so I can stop being bored?"

"No, Dez," he says, holding me. "I told you that people won't be willing to invest in you unless you invest in yourself. You stepped out of your comfort zone and launched your business last year; you also made a good profit. That was enough to convince me to invest in you. This is your place—my name isn't even on the deed. This is my Valentine's Day gift to you." Justin smirks at me then. "Plus, some chocolate covered strawberries and other treats back at the condo."

Chuckling, I throw my arms around him. He hugs me and kisses my forehead.

"I don't know what to say," I admit, crying into his chest.

"Say you have a couple of names lined up for this building. Say you wanna decorate this place. Say you're open to strawberry syrup."

I laugh while playfully hitting him. "And you *bought* this? How are you going to afford this and the building you're leasing?"

"My lease on that is up in July. By then, I should be moved into my new three-story building a couple of blocks from here."

I look up at him with my mouth wide open. He shrugs.

"I'm finna open a law firm. I'll hire attorneys and paralegals, legal assistants—the whole works. It's time for both of us to move forward in our careers."

"This is scary."

"New seasons can be scary, but that doesn't mean we shouldn't do it," he comforts.

I kiss his cheek as we remain holding one another.

"There are three rooms, one office, and two more bathrooms in the back, but it's late. Why don't we come by in the morning, so you can get a true feel for the place."

Nodding, I turn to exit. "Did you remember to stop by the pharmacy?" I ask as he turns off the light.

He smacks his forehead as the door closes behind us. "My bad, Dez, I forgot."

"Good," I smirk, walking ahead.

I see Justin lick his lips from my periphery. He quickly locks the building and hurries behind me.

Epilogue: Justin

November 24, 2017

"Come back to bed, babe," I groan when I don't feel Dez beside me.

"I'm late," she calls, flushing the toilet.

I grab my phone and look at the time. "Late for what? It's only eight in the morning."

She remains silent while washing her hands. Sighing, I get out of bed and drag my feet to the bathroom. "Late for what? A photoshoot?" I ask.

Dez gives me a worried look while holding a white stick. I walk to the toilet confused as to why she's surprised that she's late. She's late to almost everything. She even writes her appointments in her planner twenty minutes early just to ensure she's on time.

"That's a weird thermometer," I note, flushing after peeing.

"It's not a thermometer, Justin." Dez's voice is high-pitched, like she's worried.

"What is it then?" I ask, washing my hands.

"A pregnancy test."

I meet her gaze through the mirror. It's been a little over a year since we've been married, and we haven't talked about kids once. Well, except when we tell people we aren't ready for them yet. We have too much fun taking sporadic trips, staying out into the wee hours of the night, and enjoying each other in every way. We followed her calendar and planned accordingly around her fertile days. Why is she taking a pregnancy test?

"How are you feeling?" I ask, putting my personal feelings aside.

"Nervous. Scared. What do I look like being a mom?"

I chuckle, and she glares at me. "Sorry," I say, smiling. "But the thought of you raising a miniature, spoiled version of you tickles me."

"I am not spoiled," she argues as the test shows less than a minute remaining.

I raise an eyebrow, and she smiles. "Guess I have to stop denying it, huh?"

I nod before grabbing a facecloth to wash my face.

"What will we do if it's positive?" Dez asks. "I mean, we can't have a baby here; there's only one bedroom. Not to mention nothing in the condo is babyproof."

"I've been telling you for months that we should move into a house. I told you about Kareem Johnson, that realtor I met."

"I don't want to leave the city though, and having a baby is definitely not a reason to. We can just get a two-bedroom in this building."

"Your husband asking to leave isn't a reason either, apparently," I say, wetting the washcloth. "Raheem was telling me about this nice house in Marietta. It has four bedrooms, three full baths, and two offices so we can each have our own. Plus, it has brick on all sides."

"No more elevator-make-out sessions, making love by the moonlight that beams through your floor-length windows, or surprise trips to wherever we want. We're supposed to be the rich aunt and uncle; let Romeo and Jane have all the babies."

The test beeps then, and Dez takes a deep breath before picking it up. She glances at me, eyes wide. I look at her and smile.

THE END